He'd been ⬚⬚⬚ ⬚ because he ⬚⬚⬚⬚⬚⬚⬚⬚⬚⬚⬚⬚ when she'd seen that shower and it had sent all kinds of wild thoughts spinning through his head.

And if he had read her right, she'd had the same kinds of ideas. And watching color infuse her face when his gaze had landed on the bed had given him a sense of satisfaction that was far too appealing. Far too dangerous.

And he'd actually been glad her mom was there, because it meant he couldn't act on any of those impulses. It had probably saved him a lot of grief in the long run. A brief romp in the bedroom was one thing, but there was something about Shanna that seemed to hint that she wasn't one to blithely have one-night stands. He wasn't sure how he knew that, but it was there in the way she didn't openly try to figure out if the attraction was mutual and then let him know she was there for the asking.

Which meant he needed to tread a lot more carefully around her.

Dear Reader,

Loss is hard. And when that loss is a parent, it can be even harder. Shanna Meadows knows this firsthand, having lost her father during military service when she was young. But she grows up loving the holiday she and her dad spent so much time preparing for: Halloween. Her love of the holiday transfers even over to her job, where she heads up a special pumpkin-carving party for some of their younger patients and their families. But there's a new doctor in town. One who has a "bah humbug" attitude toward Halloween that presents a challenge. Yet as she learns more about him, an attraction grows and blooms. Except Shanna doesn't know everything, and when she finds out more, it sends her into a tailspin.

Thank you for joining Shanna and Zeke as they navigate waters that are emotionally charged and that leave them both with some hard choices to make: take a chance on love or walk away forever. I hope you love their story as much as I loved writing it!

Love,

Tina Beckett

RESISTING THE BROODING HEART SURGEON

—

TINA BECKETT

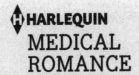

HARLEQUIN

MEDICAL
ROMANCE

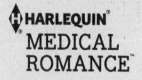

Recycling programs
for this product may
not exist in your area.

ISBN-13: 978-1-335-59500-3

Resisting the Brooding Heart Surgeon

Copyright © 2023 by Tina Beckett

Harlequin Enterprises ULC
22 Adelaide St. West, 41st Floor
Toronto, Ontario M5H 4E3, Canada
www.Harlequin.com

Printed in U.S.A.

Three-time Golden Heart® Award finalist **Tina Beckett** learned to pack her suitcases almost before she learned to read. Born to a military family, she has lived in the United States, Puerto Rico, Portugal and Brazil. In addition to traveling, Tina loves to cuddle with her pug, Alex, spend time with her family and hit the trails on her horse. Learn more about Tina from her website or friend her on Facebook.

Books by Tina Beckett

Harlequin Medical Romance

California Nurses
The Nurse's One-Night Baby

Starting Over with the Single Dad
Their Reunion to Remember
One Night with the Sicilian Surgeon
From Wedding Guest to Bride?
A Family Made in Paradise
The Vet, the Pup and the Paramedic
The Surgeon She Could Never Forget

Visit the Author Profile page
at Harlequin.com for more titles.

To my dad, who loved serving his country

PROLOGUE

SHANNA MEADOWS HEARD the sound first, before she fully comprehended what it was. Her mom was crying. Loudly. She slowly made her way toward the living room, realizing she was late for school. She hadn't meant to oversleep, didn't even remember her mom trying to wake her up.

The legs of the giraffe pajama bottoms she'd gotten last Christmas were still a little too long, and they dragged across the carpet with every step she took as she moved closer and closer to the sound. Maybe she should go back to her room and get dressed. Even if she was late, her mom could still take her to school.

Her dad had told her she needed to help around the house while he was gone, and she'd tried. She'd really tried. But now her mom was sobbing, and she could hear another voice in the room talking to her. A man's voice.

It wasn't her dad's. She was suddenly scared.

She came into the room and saw two men in uniforms, like the ones her dad wore on special occasions. "Ma'am, we want you to know that your husband was a hero. His sacrifice saved the lives of his troop."

Sacrifice? What did that mean?

Her mom's eyes suddenly swung her way, spotting her in the doorway. She dabbed at her eyes, which were really red and had a weird expression in them. "G-go back to bed, baby."

"But I'm late for school. Is something wrong with Dad?"

The two men stood like statues, not saying anything, but one of them glanced at the other.

Her mother closed her eyes for a second before looking at her again, drawing a deep breath as if she, too, was really scared about something. "You're not going to school today, Shan."

Not going to school? She always went to school unless she was really sick or there was too much snow on the ground. "But why?"

"Go back to bed, and I'll come talk to you in a few minutes."

As she looked into the unsmiling faces of the two men, who hadn't even said hello to her, Shanna realized something was very wrong. Something more wrong than not getting up in time to catch the school bus. And it had something to do with her dad. With the word *sacrifice* the men had used.

Suddenly, she *wanted* to go back to bed. To go back to sleep and wake up all over again. Wake up to the normal sounds of her mother getting breakfast ready and hollering that she needed to hurry.

Wake up to her mother *not* crying.

A normal day.

But today wasn't normal. And from the way her mom looked, and the way Shanna was feeling, days weren't going to feel normal again for a very long time.

If ever.

CHAPTER ONE

SHANNA PASSED THE wall commemorating military service at Everly Memorial Hospital and averted her eyes. It was a great acknowledgment of staff members' service, both current and past, but it tended to jar her every time she saw it. She normally tried to avoid this particular corridor, as it pulled at the cloak of positivity she tended to wear for her patients. For her mom, back when they were both grieving Shanna's dad's death. The word *sacrifice* still had the ability to rock her world, since she'd learned that her dad had found and attempted to defuse a pipe bomb found inside a box of food supplies and had been killed in the process. But he had saved lives that day. She and her mom had gone through some very hard times right after her dad's death, and her mom had never married again. Shanna didn't think that would ever change.

She couldn't blame her. After all, she was pretty wary of relationships, too, after watching her mom descend into a depression so deep that she'd had to be hospitalized after her husband's death. Shanna had gone to live with her grandmother while her mother received treatment, but the terror of somehow losing her mom, too, had never completely healed. She never wanted to live through a pain like that again.

She hurried down the hallway toward the elevator, away from the prints. She was a little late for work, which was almost unheard of for her, but traffic had been horrible today with an accident bringing the line of cars to a standstill.

Once on her floor, Maura, one of the nurses and a good friend, grinned at her. "I never thought I'd see the day Shanna Meadows was late."

"Ugh! Traffic was awful. How's it been today?"

"Actually pretty quiet. You have time to sneak away for a piece of cake for that new doctor we're getting, if you want. It's in the break room."

"Cake?"

Maura laughed. "I thought that might perk you up a bit. You looked a little sad when you got off that elevator."

She forced her face into a mock scowl. "Just irritated at some of the crazy drivers out there."

"Go get cake. It'll make you feel better. And bring me a piece, too, while you're at it, if you don't mind."

Maybe a dose of sugar really would help chase the weird sense of melancholy away. Or at least help her put on a happier face. "I don't mind a bit. I'll be back in just a minute or two."

With that, she pivoted and punched the button to call the elevator she'd just exited. The doors opened immediately. Wow, it really was quiet, if no one else had summoned the thing. She could only hope the day stayed that way.

"Dr. Vaughan, welcome to Everly Memorial Hospital."

The paper plates surrounding a large

rectangular cake was evidently something they did for every new staff member, but it seemed weird somehow. He wasn't used to any kind of fanfare when he'd changed duty stations in the army. It was simply part of what was expected of you.

He smiled at Dan Brian, the hospital administrator, bypassing the cake and opting for a cup of coffee instead. People filed in and out, grabbing slices and murmuring their own words of welcome before heading back out to the floor. Actually, Zeke was anxious to get out there and join their ranks.

A stack of papers next to the coffeepot caught his attention, and he glanced at the Mark Your Calendars heading before perusing the rest of the flyer.

The hospital was evidently hosting a pumpkin-carving party for Halloween sponsored by a local charity as a fundraiser and to help boost community awareness of what Everly had to offer. His brows went up as he saw the words "All staff members are encouraged to attend." From his experience, "encouraged" was a euphemism for "expected." The party was planned for the day before Halloween, probably so that people with kids could still participate in their neighborhood activities on the thirty-first.

Great. The event was only two weeks away. He'd hoped to be able to stay low-key until he got a feel for the way the hospital ran. He was pretty sure it was nothing like his last post in Pensacola. Not that he missed it particularly. It held a mixture of memories both good and bad. But at least he'd been able to leave the area where his ex-fiancée still lived. The few times he'd run into her over the last couple of years, the encounters had been awkward. Kristen was now married with a baby. And her husband was definitely *not* associated with the military.

Yes, he'd been happy to move. Happy to be able to make the decision on his own, with no arguing, no debates, no negotiating. And his sense of relief at finally being able to shake off the shadows of his past was surprisingly strong. He was hoping to convince his parents to relocate from Jacksonville, since there were some wonderful specialists here in the Tampa area. It was part of the reason he'd chosen the city.

Compared with what his dad was going through, having to attend a pumpkin-carving party seemed a pretty minor inconvenience. As long as he didn't have to carve one himself.

He picked one of the flyers up and folded it, tucking it into the pocket of his lab coat.

Dan evidently saw the move and said, "We hope you'll join us for that. The kids have an absolute ball at it."

Zeke smiled. "How could I say no?"

"It's fun. I promise. Have you gotten settled in your office yet?"

He wasn't much for Halloween. It wasn't that he didn't like it. He'd just never been one for costumes or parties. "Not yet. I was just trying to remember where it was. If you'll just point me in the right direction…"

Dan started to say something, then the door opened, and a woman entered. Her hair was glossy black and hung straight, sliding like silk over her shoulders. Her eyes met his for a second before skipping past him to look at something on the table.

The cake, probably.

The administrator's brows went up. "Perfect. Shanna, would you mind coming over here for a minute?"

The woman's easy smile swung back their way. "Sure thing." Dark brown eyes met his again. "I take it we have you to thank for these tasty treats." She held out her hand. "Shanna Meadows. I'm a respiratory therapist and nurse here at Everly."

"Nice to meet you. I'm Zeke Vaughan. Cardiothoracic surgeon. And you all have a way of making a guy feel welcome."

She laughed. "If that's all it takes to win you over, then consider every day to be cake day."

No one could be that cheerful all the time. Or was she merely doing it for Dan's benefit?

As if hearing his thoughts, the other man smiled. "Shanna is actually in charge of making our Halloween party the successful community outreach endeavor that it's been over the five years she's been with us." He paused and glanced at her. "Have you had cake yet?"

"Nope. That's what I snuck in here for." She tossed a lock of hair over her shoulder.

"Can I talk you into getting it to go and have you show Dr. Vaughan to his office and fill him in on the party? I'm meeting with members of the board in a few minutes."

"Of course." She bypassed the plates that already had some pre-sliced sections on them and cut her own piece. A chunky one. And then she cut a second slice.

For later?

That made him smile, for some reason. If she was peeved that she was going to have to entertain him for the next fifteen minutes or so, she didn't show it.

"Ready?" she asked. "Ever been to a costume party before?"

Costumes? Had the brochure mentioned that? "Um…not since elementary school."

She started to push the door open before stopping and turning toward him, somehow managing to hold both the door and her plates. "You're kidding, right?"

Okay, so maybe Zeke was the one who should be peeved. But he wasn't. There was something infectiously happy about Shanna Meadows. Something that made him want to take a minute or two longer to get to his office.

Now *that* peeved him. There was no way in hell he was going to let his thoughts circle around her. The sooner he shook her off, the better. But he was going to have to do it in a way that didn't offend her. Because it wasn't her. It was him.

One side of his mouth twisted up. Wasn't that a classic breakup line?

"I'm actually not the biggest fan of trick or treat. I'm just never home."

She finished pushing the door open, holding it for him to pass through. Then, still holding both plates in one hand, she somehow managed to spear a piece of her cake and pop it into her mouth as she approached the elevator. "And when you are home, I bet your porch lights are off."

"Huh?"

"You know. To make kids think you're not home."

When she said it like that, she really did make him feel like some old curmudgeon who ran little kids off his property just for kicks.

"Nope. I don't."

He just didn't answer the door. Not because he was mean. He just…forgot what day it was and normally didn't have candy in the house.

"Well, that's good to know."

They got to the elevator and waited as it ticked down floors, headed in their direction. He nodded at the cake. "Good?"

"The best. Everyone swears by this grocery chain's sheet cakes, and they are right." The elevator stopped and they got on.

Yes, he remembered that from his childhood when his dad was stationed at Naval Air Station Jacksonville in northern Florida. When Zeke chose to join the army rather than the navy, his dad wasn't mad or upset. Instead, they often had verbal skirmishes that ended in laughter. He still missed those jokes and fun times. His dad was in the advanced stages of Alzheimer's disease. He and his mom were still in Jacksonville. It was where his father had loved serving his country. It was one of the reasons he'd chosen to retire from active duty a year ago and become a reservist. So he could spend time with his dad whenever he wanted.

He only realized Shanna had finished her cake and said something to him when the doors to the elevator reopened onto the fourth floor. He waited until she stepped off before following her. "Sorry, I missed that."

"Any idea what kind of pumpkin you'll carve?" She dumped her empty plate and fork into a nearby receptacle. "I try to keep track, so we don't have too many Baby Sharks—as in the children's song—in the competition."

"Carve?"

She looked at him like he had two heads. "Do you like to do a traditional jack-o'-lantern? Something elaborate? Spooky?"

"I thought we were just there for moral support while the kids carved them."

She stopped in front of a door. "Well, we are. But the staff also like to have a lineup of lit pumpkins. Before we help them carve their own. And the kids love going down that lineup and voting for their favorites."

"Surely in a hospital this big, not everyone participates."

"No, not everyone. And as for the size, you're right. Which is why a lot of departments team up to do one, or friends might band together and come up with a design."

And since Zeke didn't know anyone here, it was going to be a little hard to just toss his name into a hat and let someone else do all the work. Not that that was his style anyway. "Good to know."

He would say he would figure something out, but since the party was only two weeks away, it was doubtful that he would be able to devise a plan that would make him look like a team player. And actually Zeke did work pretty damn well in a team. After all, the military had ingrained that in him.

"I could help, if you wanted." As soon as the words came out, something in her face shifted and he wondered if she wanted to retract them. But despite his earlier thoughts about needing to avoid her, he was willing to jump at anything that was offered. Even if it came from a woman who set his nerves on edge.

"Aren't you already on a team?"

"I normally don't carve anything since I'm in charge of the party." She nodded at the door in front of them. "This is your office."

He took out a key ring on which he'd slipped the key Dan had given him. He slid the key into the lock and opened the door. "Isn't that a little hypocritical?"

"Excuse me?" Her head tilted and she fixed him with a narrow-eyed glance.

He'd meant it as a joke, but it had evidently gone off target. "Sorry, I was teasing. I was talking about not carving a pumpkin. And since you don't carve one, do you have any suggestions of a team I could join?"

She moved inside his office and sat down in one of the chairs, even before he had the light on. He hurriedly switched it on and watched her nose wrinkle as she looked around the small space.

"What?"

"I thought they would have given you the suite that your predecessor had."

"They offered. I told them I didn't need anything elaborate." He went behind his desk and sat in the chair. "I don't plan on spending the majority of my time here."

She looked at him for a minute as if he'd surprised her somehow. "I'll tell you what. If you buy a pumpkin, I'll help you carve it. I realize it's short notice on top of everything else you have to get used to."

"Don't feel like you have to." Although, he hoped she would. He certainly didn't want patients judging his surgical skills by his lack of talent in carving a pumpkin. Doing surgery on a human being was worlds apart from cutting into a pumpkin and hoping it came out as something recognizable.

"I don't *have* to do anything. I want to. I need to go see my next patient, so if you have any spare time today, we can get together and discuss some options."

Options for carving a pumpkin. This hospital took this a little too seriously, in his opinion. Or maybe it wasn't the hospital that did. Maybe it was the woman in charge of it who did.

Behind that cheerful exterior he thought he'd caught glimpses of a quiet intensity, although he could be mistaken about that. But something about it intrigued him. Was there more to Shanna Meadows than what she showed to the world?

It didn't matter if there was. He wasn't here to try to solve puzzles other than the ones his patients presented.

"I actually don't have any patients scheduled as Dan thought I should just try to get settled in today and then start tackling my job tomorrow. I already have a bypass surgery scheduled."

"I know. Mr. Landrum. He was admitted this morning. I'm going to assess his breathing and do a treatment on him to try to keep his oxygen levels up until he can get the bypass tomorrow. He's actually who I was getting ready to go see. I just need to drop this piece of cake off at the nurses' desk."

Ah, so it hadn't been for her.

"Who ordered the treatment?" He wasn't sure what the protocol was in the civilian world, since he'd been working in military hospitals his entire career.

"Dr. Petrochki, since his last day was yesterday afternoon."

"There are a few other cardiologists who have hospital privileges, are there not?"

"Yes, but they don't reside at the hospital." She smiled, the act making her eyes light up. "And before you ask, no, they don't have to carve pumpkins. That privilege is reserved for hospital staff. Like you."

"Lucky me," he muttered.

She actually laughed at that one. The throaty sound went right through him, as did the way her head tipped back, revealing a long length of neck.

He swallowed, trying to banish the sudden jolt of awareness that went through him. Hell, he hadn't had that happen in quite a while.

"It's a pretty popular event," she said. "Some of the surrounding doctors have been trying to get carving privileges along with their hospital privileges. Anyway, we can talk later, Mr. Landrum is waiting."

"Mind if I tag along, so I can meet him?"

"I think that might be a good idea, actually, if you're okay with starting your job today."

"The sooner the better." He stood and

picked up the lanyard that had been laid on his desk and put it around his neck. "Since I still don't know where anything is located, can you lead the way?"

"Of course." With that she got up and slid from the room with a grace that had him scrambling to set himself to rights once again.

He'd been down the path of hospital romance once before. He didn't want to venture down that road again. Thankfully, Kristen had received an offer from a nearby civilian hospital soon after they broke up and had moved on. To a new life. A new partner. And he wouldn't have had it any other way. The trick now was to not make the same mistakes he'd made with her. Which meant that any weird vibrations that he got from Shanna Meadows had to be firmly placed in the nearest trash receptacle before they had a chance to take hold and root themselves in his head. And that's exactly what he was going to do.

They dropped off the cake to Maura, who eyed Zeke with speculation when she introduced him to her. Something about that irked her and she wasn't sure why. As did having the surgeon dog her steps. She knew that it was only natural for him to want to meet the patient he'd be operating on tomorrow, but something about him made her edgy. Something that had nothing to do with the party. She wasn't sure if it was the short, crisp hair that was slicked back from his head or his ridiculously straight posture, but he reminded her of someone. Someone she liked. She just couldn't put her finger on who that might be. His general apathy toward Halloween and the pumpkin-carving contest—something that she looked forward to every year—should have rubbed her the wrong way. Instead, she'd found it amusing, a challenge, even.

There was no way she wanted anyone at the hospital to think she was showing Everly's newest doctor any kind of favoritism by helping him. Maura had already raised a brow at her when she saw the new doctor. What would she do if she found out she'd offered to help Zeke?

It really wasn't fair to expect him to jump

into his job and have time left over for something like the Halloween party. There were fourteen pumpkins already slated to be in the contest and Zeke's would make fifteen, the largest number yet. Dan was certainly happy with the way the party was making a splash in the community at large.

Mr. Landrum's room was in the cardiac care unit, which was on the same floor as Zeke's office and would make it easier for the hospital's resident doctor to do rounds. So before she could dissect her conversation with Zeke too terribly much, they'd arrived at the patient's room.

She turned back to glance at the surgeon, who'd grown silent behind her. "Ready?"

"Whenever you are."

With that, she took a deep breath and pushed through the door.

Their patient was lying propped up in bed, a cannula under his nose delivering a much-needed boost in oxygen.

"Good morning, Mr. Landrum. I brought you a visitor." She tipped her head sideways to nod at Zeke. "This is Dr. Vaughan. He'll be doing your surgery tomorrow."

Denny Landrum, at just fifty years old, had a strong wiry frame, but right now he was pale and ill-looking, and no wonder. He'd been working his butt off in his landscaping business, until chest pains had derailed him and driven him to find the reason for it. It was a good thing he had. Because he was almost 100 percent occluded in two major vessels. Once he got the surgery, he should feel like a new man. At least that was the hope.

Zeke stepped forward and pulled out a stethoscope from his jacket pocket. "Nice to meet you. Mind if I have a listen?"

"Go ahead."

Shanna watched as Zeke went through the examination. She'd seen this done literally hundreds of times before with different doctors, but there was something about how intent Zeke was as he listened to the man's chest, the furrows between his brows deepening in concentration. His expression made her shiver. To combat the sensation, she crossed her arms over her chest and went through a mental checklist of things she needed to do during the man's breathing treatment once Zeke was finished.

She kind of hoped he left while she worked, but had a feeling that hope was going to be crushed. Because he seemed like a very hands-on type of physician.

Except when it came to things not involving patients. Like pumpkin-carving parties.

Well, he was going to learn that Everly Memorial took every part of its commitment to patients seriously. And that included mental and emotional care as well, which was where the thought behind the October event had come about: keeping morale of both patients and staff up with a fun activity.

Even though Zeke didn't seem like he needed anything to help him do that. Although looks could be deceiving. She hardly knew the man well enough to know what went on in his head, or what he was truly committed to, outside of his patients. She swallowed. And not all commitments came with happy, morale-lifting endings. Hadn't her dad's commitment to his military career led to his death?

This wasn't the same thing at all. Zeke's commitment to his patients wouldn't do that. Because he was a civilian and not likely to be dragged into a situation that was supposed to be keeping the peace but had ended up painting a target on the back of every man in his unit.

Zeke pulled his stethoscope from his ears and smiled. "Are you ready to feel better?"

"Yes. Whatever it takes. I have a wife and grandchild that are counting on me." He nodded at the table next to his bed, where a framed picture sat.

The surgeon smiled and went around to pick up the picture, studying it. "Who's who?"

"That's my wife on the left, my daughter and my three-year-old granddaughter. They're living with us right now. She had to…get away…leave a bad relationship."

Shanna's heart jolted. She hadn't known that. And the inference was that the relationship had been something worse than merely not being able to get along. Her fingers tightened around the treatment packet she held in her hand. Shanna knew the type.

She'd seen them come through the hospital, periodically. Bruises and breaks that were explained away as accidents.

She couldn't imagine being a counselor tasked with unraveling the pain of betrayal and helping their patients find the courage to leave the situation. Or help a devastated wife deal with the loss of her husband to a senseless act. But she was thankful for them. Thankful that just such a specialist had helped her mom start looking outward again.

Time to put her mind back on her patient, since Zeke was returning the framed print to the table.

"Well, we're going to try to make sure you're there for them." He glanced at Shanna. "I think we have a breathing treatment that should help to clear out any congestion in your lungs."

"Shanna has been great. As has Dr. Petrochki. I was kind of hoping he could do my surgery—no offense. But he's evidently retiring."

Zeke smiled at him, seemingly unruffled by the fact that the man had basically said he'd rather have his former cardiologist perform his bypass. "He is. And I'd better hope I can live up to Dr. Petrochki's standards, then, hadn't I? I'll do my best not to disappoint you."

As if realizing how what he'd said sounded, Mr. Landrum was quick to say, "That didn't come out right, and I'm sorry."

"It's completely understandable. Do you have any questions I can help answer?"

He seemed to take a minute to think. "How long do I have to stay in the hospital after the surgery? It's busy season with lawn care right now. But then again, we're in Florida where it's always busy season."

"I'm thinking we'll need to keep you about a week. But as far as your business goes, do you have someone who can run it for a bit? You'll need to take it easy for the next six weeks to allow the grafted vessels to heal."

"I have a neighbor who's a landscape architect. He's going to take on the clients who need to keep to a set schedule. The rest we're trying to stretch out the times between cuts until I'm back up to speed.

I wish the old ticker had given me some advance warning, so I could have planned better."

Zeke touched his arm. "It did give you advance warning. You were very lucky."

Mr. Landrum's face cleared. "I hadn't really thought about it like that. But I guess you're right. Thank you."

The cardiologist glanced at Shanna, who felt kind of shell-shocked. His bedside manner was better than she expected it to be. Dr. Petrochki was a lot gruffer and tended to brush patients' concerns away. But he was very good at what he did.

"Are you ready?" he asked.

"Oh…yes." Feeling his eyes on her, she finished getting everything together and moved toward their patient and started his treatment.

CHAPTER TWO

SHANNA MEADOWS HAD been very good at her job. Earlier today as he watched her adeptly give the treatment, talking to Mr. Landrum as if he were a close friend and not just a patient, he could guess that she was probably as popular with her charges as Dr. Petrochki evidently was.

But partway through the therapy, it had started feeling like he was spying on her, so he'd given her a nod and had gone back to his own office to look at Mr. Landrum's chart, mentally agreeing with the workup and planning that his predecessor had done. He'd been very thorough, down to marking the location of the vessels he would have used for grafts, even though he'd already known he wouldn't be the one doing the surgery. He'd saved their patient a lot of time, since Zeke didn't have to repeat all of the diagnostic tests.

He glanced at his watch. He was supposed to meet Shanna for lunch in the courtyard to discuss the party. He probably should have insisted that they meet during working hours so she wasn't having to use her personal time to discuss hospital business, but she'd said she really didn't have a break in her schedule today, and since his would be filling up starting tomorrow, the sooner they met, the better for both of them.

He headed down to the ground floor, where the courtyard was, and went through the cafeteria line, picking out a sandwich and bowl of soup before exiting to the outside. Tampa's heat and humidity hit him almost immediately, but the shade of the palm trees in the outdoor dining area made it bearable.

Shanna waved to him from across the way. He headed over to her and sat down on the concrete bench across from her. She'd chosen a fruit bowl and salad. "No cake this time?"

"No cake. I already had my daily dose of

sweets, so I'm going to be good for a couple of days." She said it with a smile that picked at something inside his chest. Something he recognized and had learned to be wary of.

What was it with her? Or maybe he should be asking what was it with *him*? He hadn't had especially strong reactions to women since his split with Kristen. And for it to start happening here…with someone he'd be working pretty closely with? Probably not a good habit to get into. Especially since he had no idea how she felt about the military. A subject that had caused so much strife with his ex.

His dad and grandfather had both been good men and had served in the navy, so Zeke's pride in military service had been instilled from a young age. Going into the army as a doctor had seemed the perfect marriage of his love of medicine and family pride. His dad's diagnosis had come just as he and Kristen had started dating, and maybe she'd been right in saying that he loved the army more than he loved her. But he couldn't just up and leave. He'd had a contract to fulfill, which Kristen just couldn't seem to grasp. And even if he could, it wasn't something he wanted to spring on his father, who was fighting his own battle. So rather than arguing, Zeke found it easier to just shut down every time the subject came up.

What he hadn't expected, however, was to come home one day to an empty house. While the loss of his dad was happening in slow, agonizing increments, Kristen had done the opposite and left him in one decisive move that had cut him to the core. Only afterward did he realize he'd probably rushed the relationship along to give his dad what he said he wanted most: to see Zeke happily married, and maybe even with a grandchild or two. He'd gotten neither. And looking back, Kristen's leaving had probably been a blessing in disguise.

His attention was yanked back to the present at the sound of Shanna flipping open a blue binder and thumbing through a couple of tabs before stopping on a page that boasted a kind of list. "Okay, so here's the chart of what teams are planning on carving for their pumpkin. We have everything from *Star Wars* to a comic book character planned. Take a look and see maybe what to avoid."

What to avoid would include not looking at her any more than absolutely necessary. So he stared at the sheet of paper instead. Hell, how on earth was he going to figure out what to carve when it seemed everything under the sun had already been chosen. How did one even carve a sunset into a pumpkin anyway?

"Do you have some kind of master list with ideas? Although I have to tell you, I'm not sure I can do much more than the traditional toothy jack-o'-lantern smile."

"Sure you can. There are all kinds of videos online of how to carve images on pumpkins. Almost anything you can imagine."

He thought for a minute. "Maybe since I'm a cardiac surgeon, I can carve some kind of heart."

Shanna's brows went up. "I take it you're not talking about this kind of heart." She formed a heart shape out of her joined hands.

Something about the symbol and the smile behind it made his gut twinge.

"Is that an option? I wouldn't need a video for that, since I think even I can saw a heart shape into a pumpkin."

"If you can do an actual heart, I think that would be super cool. And educational. And it would certainly fit a hospital setting along with a cardiologist." She pulled her phone out and looked at something. "How about along these lines?"

Surprisingly, there was a simple anatomic heart carved into a pumpkin. And it looked like it might actually be doable. Not like something that might require an engineering degree and special tools. "Can you send me that picture?"

"Sure? What's your number?"

He gave it to her and waited for a second as she punched something into her own phone. Then his pinged.

Only afterward did he wonder if it was a good idea for them to have each other's numbers.

Why not? It wasn't like they were going to be texting each other late into the night. Or that she would ever form a heart with her hands and mean anything by it other than work. This was not personal. He tried to remember exactly how things had started up with Kristen, but it was kind of a blur. They'd met at medical school, but he couldn't remember when things had changed from them being acquaintances to something deeper. Or maybe he'd blocked out a lot of the experience or maybe his dad's failing memory had superseded all other recollections from that time.

He knew one thing, though: continuing that relationship after it became obvious Kristen wanted a civilian doctor whose earning capabilities were far greater than that of a military doctor hadn't been his brightest moment. But it was a cautionary tale. He certainly didn't want to change hospitals again because of a relationship. Not that he'd actually done that last time. He'd simply gotten out of active duty when his contract was up and had chosen to leave his military hospital, which was ironic, seeing as that's what Kristen had wanted in the first place. Getting out of the area had simply been a nice side benefit, although he'd liked living in the Panhandle of Florida.

He glanced at the photo of the carved pumpkin. "I think maybe this is the one I'll do."

"Okay, I'll mark it down." She jotted something in her notebook.

He took a bite out of his tuna salad, finding it surprisingly tasty. Or maybe he was still used to military food, which tended to be bare-bones, since it normally focused on feeding large numbers of service people at once.

Studying her for a minute, he wondered how she'd become interested in respiratory therapy, although it was probably for the same reason any of them entered their specialty. Something piqued their interest and made them want to take a closer look. That had certainly been how it had been with him and cardiothoracic medicine. His biology classes had gone over the respiratory system and he'd been fascinated by how oxygenated blood was pushed through the body. The rest had been history.

His grades had been good enough to get him into medical school, and by choosing the military route, the army had basically paid for his education with the agreement that he would put in the time with the armed forces. It had been the perfect combination. He wouldn't change anything if he could. Other than his failed romance. He'd dated since then but had made sure they were both on the same page. He wasn't interested in anything serious. And at thirty-nine, he wasn't sure he ever would be. And his dad's memory was much worse now. At some point he would need round-the-clock care, which was another reason he hoped his mom would agree to move to Tampa.

"So tell me something good and something not so good about working at Everly."

He wasn't sure why he had asked the question, but it seemed like a fairly impersonal topic. He'd expected choosing a subject to carve into his pumpkin to take longer than it had. But it seemed rude to pick up his tray and move to another table, even if it was just to give her some time to herself.

She snapped her binder shut. "That's a hard question. Not the 'good' part, because there are really a lot of those. The hospital is good to its staff. At least that has been my experience. There's not much turnover and there are quite a few doctors who want in. As for the bad…maybe just the normal hospital soap opera stuff. It's obviously not in league with some of the television shows that depict everyone sleeping with everyone else, but there is an element of that that goes on in almost every setting."

Yes, he had experienced that firsthand. And knowing it went on here as well was a good warning to watch his step. He didn't want to be tangled up in any of that. Especially not this early after his arrival. Not that he wanted it at all. Kristen had proved to be a good inoculation against relationships.

"You're right. That seems to happen almost everywhere."

"So you've experienced it?"

This was one question he didn't really want to answer. "Let's just say it went on at the hospital I was at as well."

"Where were you?"

"At a hospital in Pensacola."

Her brows went up. "That's quite a change. Why Tampa?"

He wasn't sure why, but he didn't want

to just vomit up everything about himself to her. The stuff about his dad's diagnosis and his previous relationship were things he rarely talked about, even to people he knew well. And to someone he barely knew? Not something he saw himself doing. Especially with some of the things he'd seen on the field. Unlike the good outweighing the bad, like Shanna had talked about, some of what he'd witnessed had been horrific. He wasn't anxious to bring up those memories, especially since it had taken time with a professional to work through some of those experiences.

Before he could think of a plausible explanation for his move, his cell phone went off. Followed almost immediately by Shanna's.

They glanced at each other before looking down at their screens. "I'm needed down in the ER. You?"

"Same."

He took one last bite out of his sandwich before taking his tray and discarding the rest of his lunch. Shanna did the same.

"Did your message give any details?"

"Nope. Yours?"

He shook his head. "No. Just that I was needed in the ER to help with a patient."

They made the short walk over to the emergency department and were flagged down by one of the nurses. "Shanna, we've got an acute respiratory distress in room one, as soon as Dr. Vaughan gets—"

"I'm Dr. Vaughan."

"Great. We're waiting on our pulmonologist to arrive at the hospital. He's been at home with a sick child and a pregnant wife. But he's en route as we speak. They're from Guatemala. Our translator isn't here yet, but Shanna speaks some Spanish, which is why we called her."

Once in the room, they found a child who was about two years old laboring to breathe, every respiration bringing a deep hacking cough that brought up thick mucus.

Zeke went into action, pulling out his stethoscope and hauling the boy's shirt over his head. He was painfully thin. Thinner than he should have been, and when Zeke glanced at the other child and the parents, they were all within normal ranges. "How long has he had this cough?"

Shanna switched to Spanish, her hands moving as she translated the question. The woman, who he assumed was the mom, responded.

"She says a few weeks. But Marco's had problems with colds for most of his life."

"How long have they been in the country?"

Shanna translated, the answer coming back as three weeks. They were visiting family and hoped to move to the States in the near future.

He could hear congestion deep in the boy's lungs, and when he did bring up sputum, it was thick, with a texture he didn't expect. It raised a few warning flags, but he didn't want to jump to conclusions. Not yet. When asked if the child ate well, the parents looked at each other before talking to Shanna.

"They said he eats, but often doesn't feel well afterward. When he was a baby, the doctors told them it was colic and that he would outgrow it. But he's not growing like their other child did."

Zeke could see that. "Let's do a breathing treatment with albuterol and add some hypertonic saline to thin the mucus, and can you have someone call down to pediatrics? I want to get a sweat test, just to rule something out."

"Sweat test?" Shanna moved closer, speaking in low tones. "Are you thinking cystic fibrosis?"

Of course she would know what he was testing for. She was a respiratory therapist. There was every chance she had seen a case of this before at a hospital this size.

"It's a possibility. Just from the sound of his lungs and the fact that he has a history of lung infections combined with what I'm thinking could be malabsorption syndrome."

Cystic fibrosis was primarily thought of as a lung disease, but it attacked more organs than just the pulmonary system. The inherited condition also affected the digestive tract with thick sticky mucus that had the ability to clog the intestines or even create blockages.

Shanna called the nurses' station before preparing the treatment that he'd asked for. When she came over with the nebulizer, she held the molded plastic over Marco's nose and mouth, soothing him in soft tones when he seemed scared. Zeke made notes in the chart. "How long are they here in the States?"

She asked the parents and then came back with "Four more weeks."

Barely time enough to come up with a diagnosis, much less a treatment plan. One that would need to be followed scrupulously. "I want to make some phone calls when we leave here to their country and find a specialist I can refer them to. Can you help with translating and find out which part of the country they're from?"

"Of course."

Zeke had dealt with a couple of cases of cystic fibrosis before during his rotation, since if breathing was compromised, the heart could grow enlarged and need help pumping efficiently.

A nurse came in. "Dr. Rogers's wife just went into labor. He's had to turn around and go back home. Are you good? Do you need me to call one of the pulmonologists who has hospital privileges?"

"Let me see how the sweat test goes, so we know a little more about what we're dealing with."

The nurse nodded. "Someone should be here with the test in a few minutes." She then withdrew.

Fortunately the albuterol was having the desired effect and opening the airways, and Marco's breathing was discernibly less rattly, the coughing already sounding a little more productive than it had a few minutes ago.

Watching Shanna move around the bed with confident purpose, having the perfect amount of compassion and steadiness, he could see what a valuable asset she was to the hospital. The fact that she'd taken on the Halloween party—had been the one to introduce the festivities to the hospital, in fact—when it only added onto what were probably long, hard days, made something tug in his midsection.

Something he tried to squash.

But then, Kristen had been good at her job, too. But that hadn't meant they were compatible. They hadn't been. Not that he was assuming a fleeting sense of attraction would derail him toward a place he'd gone before. And hell, he'd just gotten to the hospital. What was he even doing thinking along these lines?

He purposely avoided looking up from his tablet, where he was typing his notes, until he heard Marco say something to his parents.

"What did he say?"

Shanna was looking at the boy with wide eyes. "He says he wants to play. And is asking if we have a train."

Zeke glanced at what Marco was pointing at on the wall. Sure enough, it was a picture of a toy train. In fact, he just realized that the entire room was decorated in colors that a child would like. He hadn't even noticed that. Maybe the hospital had different exam rooms geared toward different age groups. That would be quite an undertaking, but from what he was learning about how the hospital was run, it shouldn't be surprising.

"I don't know if we have a train or not. We used to have toys in the pediatric waiting rooms, but when COVID hit, they stored most of those away. I don't think they've brought them back yet, but let me go get one of the coloring packets that we keep for children."

"Thanks."

Yes, she was definitely an asset. As soon as the thought skipped through his head, he gritted his teeth. As were all of the staff who worked at the hospital.

While she was gone, another nurse came in with the sweat test. She was also good at her job. She didn't speak Spanish but was able to get across what she needed through pantomime. By the time Shanna came back with a colorful little plastic bag, the nurse had the solution that would promote sweating swabbed on the boy's arm and was waiting to collect some of the fluid.

"Everything going okay?"

"Fine." He realized his word was shorter than it should have been when Shanna looked at him with a frown. Probably wondering what he was so peeved at.

It wasn't her. It was him.

Hell, it was the same phrase he'd used earlier when thinking about her, and he didn't like it. At all.

But, more than likely he would be working with her on a regular basis even after Halloween was long gone, and unless he wanted to pack up shop every time someone caught his eye, he was going to have to learn how to deal with it. One way or another.

"Okay, I think that about does it," the nurse said. "I'll get this right over to the lab. We should have results within the hour, unless they're backed up with something else."

"Perfect, thanks."

Once she left, Shanna turned to him. "Do you want to keep them in the exam room? There's actually a small waiting room just to the back of the department, if you think they would be more comfortable there."

"Is that what normally happens in cases like these?"

"Yes, in case we get a sudden influx of patients who need rooms."

He nodded. "Let's do that, then." He glanced at what she was holding in her hand. "Maybe that will keep him occupied while they wait."

"I'll take them," she said.

"Thank you. I'll go see if we can pull a pulmonologist in from somewhere, since I have a feeling the results are going to show CF. I'll check on a genetic counselor as well, since if he does have the condition, they'll want to make informed decisions about having any more children from here on out."

Before Marco and his family fell completely off his radar, he wanted to make sure they knew about the Halloween party, so he reminded himself to mention it to them.

Seriously? Since when was he thinking this party was a good thing?

Since he'd met a little boy who needed something good on his horizon, since life was about to get much more complicated and was likely to stay that way forever.

It had nothing to do with Shanna, who was supposed to help him carve his own pumpkin. At least that was what he was choosing to believe.

CHAPTER THREE

"I NEED SUCTION!"

The second Mr. Landrum's heart re-started, his surgical field was covered in blood. Zeke went into crisis mode, trying to figure out where the blood was coming from. The surgical nurse's suction cleared a path for him to see long enough to tell that the first grafted vein was fine. But the second... Hell, the return of circulating blood had blown a hole straight through it. He hadn't nicked it, had checked it over before suturing it in place. There had to have been a hidden weak spot in it.

"Clamp! And let's get him back on by-pass."

A clamp was slapped in his hand almost immediately and he closed off the vessel, promptly stopping the flow of blood. If it had been a small leak, he could have sutured it shut, but even though the vein had passed their precheck to make sure it could hold fluid, there was always the possibility that an imperfection had gone unnoticed.

They were going to have to redo the graft with one of the others they'd harvested. Hell!

He barely noticed someone swabbing sweat off his forehead as the whir of the bypass machine took over. They'd harvested enough length from Mr. Landrum's saphenous vein that they could redo the bypass. He just hated to have the patient on the heart-lung machine any longer than necessary.

Working as quickly as he could, he undid the faulty graft and prepared to replace it. And God… He hoped there were no more surprises.

Shanna checked at the nurses' desk for what seemed like the umpteenth time. She'd been expecting a call to do a breathing treatment on Zeke's bypass patient, Matthew Landrum. But so far, he hadn't come out of surgery yet. And it had been six hours, longer than most of the bypasses she'd been involved with had taken.

Had something happened?

Lord, she hoped not. Not just because Mr. Landrum was a genuinely nice guy. But also because it was Zeke's first surgery at the hospital, and for some reason she wanted it to be a successful one.

Why? She should hope that all of the hospital's surgeries were successful.

And she did. This one just seemed...different.

Because of the surgeon?

No, of course not. His periodic glances her way may have sent her heart racing in her chest, but it was more than that. She had a feeling the surgeon would take it very hard if Mr. Landrum didn't pull through.

He'd already had to break the hard news to young Marcos's family yesterday afternoon that the child did indeed have cystic fibrosis. And even though treatment options over the years had increased life expectancies, it was still a life-altering diagnosis.

And Marcos would need specialized care his entire life.

His face, as he'd explained the situation and as she'd translated, had been tense, his eyes on Marcos, who'd been busy coloring a train.

And then he'd told the family about the pumpkin-carving party, which had actually shocked her, asking if she had a flyer the family could take with them.

Her eyes had met his and there had gone her heart, pounding like crazy in her chest. It was a ridiculous reaction, and she'd taken the opportunity to murmur that she would go get one of the pamphlets. Once outside the door, she'd leaned against it for several seconds to catch her breath before heading for the information desk, where a stack of notices for the Halloween party were kept.

Shaking off the memories and wanting to do something besides just thinking of what had happened yesterday, she decided to actually walk through the doors where the surgical suites were housed, since she was between patients at the moment. She didn't know what that was going to accomplish, since she didn't have X-ray vision. In reality, she just needed something to do besides hang out at the nurses' desk.

One of the doors to Surgical Suite One opened and a nurse came out looking somber.

Oh, no! Something *had* happened.

Then Zeke came out, tugging his surgical mask down as he did. He didn't look much happier than the nurse had.

"Zeke..." Her voice faded away, unsure of what she could really say or do that would make him feel any better.

His glance swung toward her, and a frown appeared between his brows.

She definitely should have hung out by the nurses' desk if his expression was anything to go by. But she was here now, and she needed to somehow explain her appearance outside the door of his operating room. "Mr. Landrum?"

"He pulled through, but he gave us a couple of scares."

"He did? Pull through, I mean? The nurse that just came out of there..."

He nodded. "It was one of her first sur-

geries, and it didn't go like clockwork. One
of the veins we harvested for the bypass had
a weak spot in it and it blew out just as we
were closing him up. We had to go back
in and stop the bleeding and redo the graft
with another portion of the vein we'd harvested. The surgery took twice as long as
we'd hoped it would, and honestly, I thought
we were going to lose him when it first went
sideways." He tugged off his cap and rolled
it up with the mask he'd removed seconds
earlier.

"But you didn't. Lose him, I mean."

"No. We didn't. Thank God." He glanced
at her again. "I need to go talk to the family,
but do you want to go get a coffee after I do?
If you don't have another patient, that is."

His frown deepened as if he hadn't been
sure why he'd made the offer. Maybe he just
didn't want to be alone, which Shanna could
totally understand. And she didn't have the
heart to say no. Especially if he needed to
talk things through.

"I don't. I was scheduled to work with Mr.
Landrum after his surgery…" She thought

fast. "Which is why I was hanging around. And yes, I would love a coffee."

"He'll need some time in recovery before that treatment. How about if I meet you by the doors to the ER in about fifteen minutes?" He hesitated again for a second. "We can talk more about the pumpkin carving."

Of course that was why he wanted to go to coffee with her. It wasn't just to decompress after a difficult surgery. Something in her deflated, and she suddenly didn't want to go with him. But she'd already said she would. To back out now would be awkward and might make him think his request for coffee had held a lot more meaning than it actually had.

No. She had to act as nonchalant as he seemed to be. "Okay, there's a coffee shop called Top Grounds around the corner. Why don't I just meet you there. You'll be close to the hospital if Mr. Landrum or the hospital suddenly needs you."

"Perfect. See you there in a few minutes."

She nodded, then turned to go, wondering what she was thinking to even consider going to coffee with him.

When she got there, the shop was busier than she'd expected it to be. She should have asked what he wanted, and she could at least order it for him. But she hadn't. But she could get hers and save a table, if there were any.

Fortunately, by the time she ordered her iced vanilla latte, a table had opened up and she snagged it, sitting down and taking a sip of her cold brew. She normally liked her coffee hot, but Tampa temperatures were steamy today, and she'd wanted something that wouldn't make her feel like she was going to melt.

She was on her second sip when she spotted Zeke entering the shop. He'd discarded his scrubs and, with his erect bearing and dark-washed jeans and a white button-down shirt, if she didn't know he was a surgeon, she would take him for an executive at some financial agency somewhere. There was no sign that he'd been engaged in a battle for someone's life not a half hour earlier. A couple of women who were at another table watched him, one of them whispering something to the other, who elbowed her, before they both giggled.

Is that how Shanna looked at him? Lord, she hoped not, although her eyes had followed his every move as well. To combat that, she turned to study the decor on the walls. All of it was coffee paraphernalia, from French presses to faded recipes that included coffee. It really was an interesting shop. One of the places she tended to frequent since it was on her way to work from her house…the one she'd spent a lot of her childhood in after her dad had died. Her mom had signed over the title a few years ago, when she decided she wanted to downsize to one of the nicer condos in the area. Being a Realtor had its perks when it came to ferreting out good deals on homes.

Her thoughts were interrupted when Zeke pulled out the chair across from her. She glanced at the table of other women and noticed one of their mouths turned down. They probably thought they were an item or something. If only they knew. But even that thought didn't completely quench the little shiver of satisfaction that he was sitting at her table and not theirs. Even though he would never be hers. Nor did she want him to be.

Was she trying to convince her libido of that? Or just giving it a heads-up that nothing was going to develop between them? Ever.

He nodded at her drink. "Cold coffee?"

She smiled at his tone and countered, "Hot day."

"Good point. It is pretty warm out there."

And yet not a hair on his head was ruffled, nor was there the slightest mark of perspiration on his crisp white shirt. If she'd had that on, she would have been dripping wet. As it was, she had a dark-patterned scrub top on for a reason. It was loose and cool and very forgiving of spilled food, drinks or sweaty days.

"Everything still okay at the hospital?" she asked.

"If you're talking about Mr. Landrum, then yes. He'd just been wheeled into recovery when I left."

"So the graft blew? Is that very common?"

He dragged a hand through his hair. "I've

never had it happen. The harvested vessel was tested and showed no signs of defects, but I'm glad it chose now to fail rather than a month or year from now. But—" a muscle worked in his jaw "—I really thought I might lose him."

She couldn't stop her hand from covering his for a second before pulling it away. "But you didn't."

"Not this time." She almost didn't hear the low mutter. Maybe he hadn't meant her to.

Had he lost another patient to something similar? She almost let the comment go by without saying anything, but there seemed to be a wealth of pain in those words. "Sometimes things just happen. Things we can't foresee or control."

Like the prick of tears behind her eyes as the thought of her dad suddenly went through her mind.

"You're right. But that doesn't mean I want it to happen on my watch."

"I get it." It sounded like something her dad would have said, and was probably what led him to try to defuse that bomb.

To shake off the thought, she added, "How is Mr. Landrum's family doing?"

"They're just glad he made it through, which I'd never had any doubt of, until the moment blood started pouring out of that vein. The vein that I'd just finished suturing in."

Maybe Zeke really had needed to talk things through. To decompress from what had almost happened. She was suddenly glad she hadn't backed out of coming.

"There was no way you could have known. And when the unthinkable happened, you were able to figure out how to fix it. That counts for a lot."

He looked at her for a long moment. "Thank you for that."

She couldn't seem to look away from him, until she saw movement at another table. The women who had ogled him were getting up to leave. Lord, maybe she really was just like them. She cleared her throat. "Do you want any changes to his treatment? As in do you still want me to do breathing treatments with him starting today? Or do you want me to wait?"

"This afternoon is fine. His aftercare will remain the same, although I'm going to do some imaging with contrast before releasing him to make sure there are no other unexpected surprises, since the replacement graft was taken from the same saphenous vein."

"You think it could fail, too?"

"Hell, I hope not. But I don't want to take any chances."

"I don't blame you. Will you keep him longer?"

He shook his head, taking a sip of his own steaming brew. "I think we'll keep him a week, like I would with most other bypass patients, and then let him finish his recovery at home. Unfortunately insurance companies don't cover cardiac rehab the way they once did, so I'll send home some detailed instructions upon discharge and hopefully get a home nurse out there who is well-versed in cardiac care."

"I could probably stop by his house on my way home to check in on him from time to time, if you think it will help."

He pursed his mouth. "I doubt his insurance would cover that."

"What if I went as a friend?"

His frown deepened. "But you're not. His friend, I mean."

She probably shouldn't have said anything. She had a feeling the hospital wouldn't really approve of her making house calls. And maybe a personal visit wouldn't even be covered under her current malpractice umbrella. She needed to check.

"I wouldn't give treatment, unless the orders were there, obviously. I was just thinking of seeing how his color and affect seemed." She wasn't sure how to retract her offer without it being weird. But she wanted to make sure that if there were problems during the healing process, they were caught early enough to be treated. After all, if her mom's descent into depression had been caught earlier, maybe she wouldn't have needed inpatient care. But there was no way to know that now. All Shanna could do was provide the best care she could for her own patients.

"Sorry if that came across wrong. I was

thinking of making sure you were compensated for your time."

"I don't do it with all of my patients, but part of my licensing covers home health treatments when needed. If I ever get tired of working in a hospital setting, I wanted another avenue available to continue practicing what I love. So far, I still get a lot of satisfaction from working with the team at Everly Memorial, though."

With no house payment, she could certainly afford to take a cut in pay if she needed to explore other options. But right now, there was no need.

"Then, as long as the hospital doesn't object, that would be great."

A warm satisfaction went through her, although it wasn't like he was patting her on the back for anything. Just expressing that he had no objections to her checking in on their patient.

Their patient.

Well… He really was, right? She was taking part in his care, no matter how small that part might be.

"Sounds good." She tried to shift gears,

since he'd been the one to mention their reason for having coffee together and she needed to steer their conversation to less personal grounds. For her own sake. "So about your pumpkin. What do you need to know?"

He stood and tucked his hand in one of his front pockets, pulling out a piece of folded paper before sitting back down. "I looked up various diagrams on hearts and came up with this. Does this look carve-able?"

She unfolded the sheet and looked at it. There was a simple pictorial image of a heart, with the major vessels coming off it. "This should be doable. We won't carve completely through the pumpkin for all of it, just through some of it, so that the light will shine through. That will give it some depth."

"Can't I just carve straight through it?" He studied it for a minute. "Wait. I think I see what you're saying. There has to be some connective tissue or it will all just fall into the pumpkin."

"Connective tissue." She laughed. "Once

a surgeon, always a surgeon. But yes. That's what I'm saying."

"And are you going to offer a class? Pumpkin Carving 101?"

"Funny you should ask that. Next week, in fact, I am offering a quick-and-dirty how-to class in the staff lounge for anyone who wants a little instruction on special techniques."

One of his brows went up. "Not that I'm asking for any special consideration or anything, but I thought you were going to help me with mine."

"I am. But what I didn't offer was to carve it for you. That wouldn't be fair to everyone else."

"You're assuming you'd win."

She smiled, thinking of the blue ribbons she'd won with her dad. "I may have won a contest or two in my younger days. But I'll admit, I've never once attempted to carve a heart—at least the organ—from one."

Even after her father had been killed, carving pumpkins had been her way of keeping his memory alive. She'd done more and more elaborate carvings as the years went by. The only reason she didn't enter her own carving in the hospital's party was that as the organizer, it seemed like a conflict of interest. So she'd been content to let other people shine. Her goal was not only to promote the hospital, but to keep the spirit of Halloween alive, something that seemed to be dying out little by little.

"When is your course?"

"Next Saturday at one p.m. Since most scheduled surgeries tended to happen on weekdays, it seemed to be the day when at least a member or two of each team would be able to come. If they need it. Some folks have been through the course before and already know what I'm going to demonstrate."

She took another pull on her straw, surprised at how much talking she'd been doing and how little drinking. Especially considering that Zeke was almost done with his own cup. How had that happened? She was never usually this talkative. She was friendly, yes. But she didn't normally monopolize the conversation. Maybe it was just to avoid talking about anything deeper.

Anything that might make her look at him the way those other women had. "Sorry. I think I've been talking way too much. Tell me more about Mr. Landrum's surgery. You said your harvested vessel came from the saphenous vein?"

"That's right. It's my preferred vein, just because the diameter tends to be closer to those of the heart. Although many surgeons use the radial artery as well. Have you seen bypass surgery?"

"Once during my training, but only because I asked to observe. I find it fascinating, although I wasn't exactly sure of what was happening from where I sat."

Zeke scooted his chair closer to hers, taking the diagram he'd brought with him and setting it on the table between them.

Her pulse immediately picked up its pace with his proximity and the light tantalizing scent of something coming from his skin. Soap? Shampoo?

He didn't seem like the type to wear cologne, although how could she know that for sure? And she wasn't going to ask him. Instead, she listened as he explained an overview of the surgery, using his finger to point out the different vessels that could be by-passed.

She could listen to those deep gravelly tones forever and never tire of them. Which was a dangerous thought, especially since she had been trying to steer the conversation clear of deep subjects. More tables in the café were now vacant besides the one with the women.

How long had she been here with Zeke, anyway?

Probably long enough. And yet she wasn't about to stop him midexplanation, so she leaned forward on the table and listened as his words painted pictures that she could visualize in her head. It was as if she were there for Mr. Landrum's surgery.

And when he finally finished, she realized she'd been holding her breath, which now whooshed out in a way that was far too loud for her liking.

He immediately glanced at her. "Sorry. I know that was long-winded."

"No, not at all. I could picture it. How on earth do you deal with the stress of surgery? Of knowing that things might not end well?"

"I try to concentrate on what I need to do, and when, and leave the rest to whoever controls life or death. Because it normally isn't me. I simply do a job and hope it's what the patient needs to survive."

"And if it's not?"

"Then the patient dies. And that's where I get stuck in my thoughts, reliving each and every move I made during surgery. Was there anything I could have done to prevent it? Was there anything the patient could have done to improve their chances for survival? Sometimes it's just the luck of the draw. No matter how hard I try. No matter how hard the patient tries to prepare... death sometimes happens. Genetics? Timing? Surgeon? There are so many variables. It's not often that we know the entire reason. Sometimes the veins are too calcified to hold sutures well or there's not a good vein or artery to harvest because of vascular disease or damage. Or there are injuries that are too devastating to overcome."

His voice hardened on that last sentence.

Probably thinking of senseless deaths caused by human violence.

"I get it. It's the same with the lungs. Sometimes there's too much damage. Or sometimes the pressure in them is too high and it eventually causes respiratory failure that no amount of treatment can prevent. Or there's cancer. Or COPD. Or any number of lung diseases."

"Like cystic fibrosis."

"Yes. Like cystic fibrosis. Thank God cases like Marcos's are not a dime a dozen. And with genetic testing, people can make informed choices about things like getting pregnant."

"So if you carried the gene, you wouldn't have children?"

"It's a recessive gene, but if my partner and I both carried the gene, I think I would choose another route, if I wanted to have a baby. Like adoption. Or donor eggs. Actually, if I carried the gene and my partner didn't, I might still choose a different avenue to become a parent, so that I didn't pass the gene on to my offspring."

"I tend to agree with you, although I

know it's each person's choice about how to handle their own genetic information." He glanced at his watch. "As fascinating as this discussion is, I'd better head back to the hospital to check on Mr. Landrum. Do you have time to do a breathing treatment, if he's awake enough to do one?"

"Yes, of course. That's why I came down to the surgery wing. I only have a couple of patients today, and fortunately nothing has come through the ER that involves breathing. So I'm available."

Almost immediately, she wished she could take back that last sentence. And from the way Zeke's eyes jerked toward her, he must have heard the unfortunate wording. But she wasn't about to stutter her way into an even bigger mess, so she pretended there was only one way her words could be construed.

"Great. Are you ready?"

Her drink was still only half-gone, but she could stick it in the staff lounge fridge and retrieve it later. "Yep. I'll bring mine with me."

They walked back to the hospital together, Shanna searching for some sort of small talk that might fill the time but coming up blank.

"Did you hook Marcos up with a lung specialist?"

"I did. One of the local pulmonologists has agreed to take him on pro bono, since the family has no medical insurance. He'll get treatments while he's here in the States." He smiled. "And his parents said he keeps pointing at the pumpkin on the flyer you gave them. I'm pretty sure they'll be here for the party."

"That's great. It'll be good to see him. And I'm so glad he'll get treatments. Were you able to find a specialist in Guatemala?"

"Not yet, but I put a call into the American consulate there, and they're checking into it."

She smiled and touched his hand again, the warmth of his skin sending a tingle through her. "Let me know if you need me to back you up or translate for you. I'd love to help that family."

There was a moment of silence after her statement.

Realizing she was still touching him, she shifted so that her arm fell back to her side, heat sliding into her face.

"I'm sure they'll appreciate that. And I might need a translator if I have to treat him again."

"I'd be happy to. Even though my family is from Cuba rather than Guatemala."

"Is the Spanish that different?"

She rocked her head from side to side. "It depends. There is a lot in common. But there are words in their version of Spanish that we don't find in our form of the language. But we can get by, for sure. And context carries a lot of cues, even when certain words are unfamiliar."

"So since your last name is Meadows, is your mom the one who's Cuban?" He stopped and frowned. "I guess Meadows could be a married name…"

"Nope. It's my maiden name. And yes, my maternal grandparents came over to this country as political refugees due to some of the civil rights violations that were going on at the time. Their last name was Gutierrez."

"So you learned Spanish from them?"

She nodded. "And my mom, who is still fluent, although she speaks English most of the time now."

They rounded the corner, and Shanna could see the hospital on the next block. It was huge, its modern white facade taking up almost an entire city block.

"Did your dad learn how to speak it as well?"

"Some." Her mouth twisted. "Unfortunately he passed away when I was ten, so I don't remember that part of him."

"I'm sorry, Shanna, I didn't mean to pry."

"You weren't. He's been gone a long time." Although the hurt and finality of his death were still things she was working through.

"Did your mom remarry?"

She shook her head. "No. He was the love of her life. I'm not sure she'll ever meet someone who can measure up to my dad."

Then they were at the hospital and entering the doors. Thankfully by that time, their conversation turned back to Mr. Landrum and his upcoming breathing treatment. And she could forget that the sensation of her fingers sliding across his hand had caused her own breathing to stop for a moment. Good thing those women from earlier had already left the coffee shop, or they might think she and Zeke really were an item.

Even though she knew for a fact that they were not. Nor would they ever be.

CHAPTER FOUR

ZEKE DIDN'T SEE Shanna for a couple of days after that first breathing treatment with Mr. Landrum. It was as if she were purposely choosing to do his therapy when Zeke wasn't around. Which was ridiculous. How would she even know when he was on the floor or doing rounds?

It was simply dumb luck that had them avoiding each other's paths. He should consider it a godsend, if anything.

Watching her animation as she talked about various things had had his eyes glued to her face, where each expression flitted across it in record time. He couldn't remember the last time he'd been that fascinated with what someone had to say, and he wasn't sure why she held him enthralled. Maybe because of the way she'd talked about heart surgeries. As if they really fascinated her, rather than it merely being politeness that had her asking about his job.

He'd never grown tired of operating on the heart. As many poems and songs that had been sung about that particular organ, it was no wonder that hearts had so many problems. They were battered and bruised by the emotions of life. And yet he'd actually found the heart was a pretty tough cookie. It could be ravaged by disease or even stress, and yes there was actually a broken heart syndrome that could be deadly, but it was a pretty resilient organ.

As if he'd summoned her, Shanna came rushing around the corner so fast that she almost careened into him. He gripped her arms to keep her from making contact with him. Probably because with his thoughts the way they were, that could prove disastrous. If her hand touching his while walking down the street could go through him like a current of electricity, imagine what body-to-body contact would do to him.

Hell. Something he did not want to think about.

"Sorry, Zeke. I'm late for Matthew Landrum's treatment after a case of acute asthma came through the ER. I just finished with it."

"Mind if I come with you? I haven't seen him since this morning and wanted to check in again before I left for the day."

"Sure. Were you able to get his imaging done?"

"It's scheduled for tomorrow. I'm hoping we can get him released by Friday."

The day before her pumpkin-carving seminar.

Now why had that thought slid through his head? One thing had nothing to do with the other.

"That's great. Isn't it sooner than you'd planned? Or did you mean a week as in a workweek?"

"No, I'd originally planned for a full seven days, but he's doing remarkably well after all he went through in surgery. He's strong and young enough to bounce back from this faster than someone in their, say, seventies or eighties. Not that I've done that many surgeries on people that old." The military didn't exactly have a thriving geriatric community in its ranks, although he had seen some older vets come through the last military hospital he'd been stationed at. It was very different from the fieldwork he'd done, where injuries from electric shock or, God forbid, things like explosive devices could cause catastrophic damage that needed lifesaving measures. Although even in the civilian world, he would surely be called on to treat some of the same things, like gunshot wounds or other types of trauma.

"Wow, being discharged that early is great news."

"Yes, it is." He noticed she didn't say anything else about going to the man's home to check on him. Had she asked the hospital about it and been vetoed? Or was she simply going to try to fly under the administration's radar and do it on her own?

"So you'll still get to come to the class on pumpkin carving?"

"I will. I have the weekend off, although I'm on call Sunday, should something urgent come into the ER."

She nodded. "Weekends can either be a

dead zone or we could be up to our eyeballs in patients."

He was personally hoping for a quiet weekend. He still needed to find an apartment or place to stay, since he'd spent this last week in one of those long-term hotel rooms. It was noisy far into the night, although it could be worse. "I'm hoping to have time to talk to a Realtor about locating more permanent living quarters."

She frowned. "Where are you now?"

"In a hotel."

Her eyes widened. "Yikes. My mom is actually a Realtor, although she's not as active as she once was. I could have her put out some feelers, unless you'd rather find someone who isn't a relative of a colleague."

"Actually, that would be great, since I don't know anyone in the area, or know who to ask about reputable Realtors in the area."

"I promise, she'll never try to strong-arm you into something you don't want. If anything, she's probably seen as too honest about the properties she comes across, but she's seen people burned on homes that turn out to be money pits. She's also a very good judge of a property's value."

"That sounds exactly what I need. How do I contact her?"

"How about I see if she's available after our carving class, and I can take you to her condo and introduce you."

He hesitated for a fraction of a second. She must have noticed because she quickly changed her words to, "Or I could just give you her phone number and let you set that up yourself. You can just tell her you work with me."

"I wasn't turning down your offer. I just don't want you to feel obligated to take me over there in person. You're already helping me with this pumpkin thing and did a great job translating for me with Marcos's parents. I don't want to seem 'extra.'"

"Extra?"

He laughed. "It's my mom's way of saying someone is being needy or a nuisance. She'll say, 'You're being a little *extra* today.' Don't tell me you've never heard that expression."

"Nope. Never." She smiled. "But I kind

of like it. And no, I don't think you're being 'extra.' You're new to the area, and a place like Tampa can seem overwhelming to people who haven't lived in tourist cities."

"I lived in the Panhandle before this, so I am a little acquainted with tourist meccas like Destin. A place that's nice to visit, but complicated to live in without getting annoyed at the constant crowds."

"I can imagine. So why on earth choose Tampa? It's pretty touristy, too."

He again hesitated over his reply, and he wasn't sure why. It just seemed that every time he mentioned being in the military people had one of two responses. Either they gushed over him, thanking him for his service, or their faces closed as if expecting him to dive into a narrative on all he'd seen and done. Kristen's face had done that a lot in the weeks before he moved out. For some reason, he didn't want to know which camp Shanna fell into. "I wanted to change locations, without completely leaving Florida. So Tampa seemed to fit the bill."

"Enough that you're ready to house hunt. Even with the Halloween party hanging over your head? You didn't seem like a fan when we met."

"I've just never been one for parties or pretending to be something I'm not." Which had been one of the problems with his ex. Even if he could have opted out of his military contract at that time, he hadn't been ready to do that, not with what his father was facing. And the military was all he'd ever known. They'd paid for his education, for God's sake. Even now he wasn't quite ready to throw it all in. The reserves were his way of having the best of both worlds.

Shanna was going to find out eventually when he had to go to a training weekend or was deployed. The hospital knew. But he'd not told any of his colleagues yet, either. Maybe he wanted to be seen as the person he was—as a surgeon—rather than some cardboard cutout that people thought military personnel were.

"I can see that about you. Your lack of pretense, I mean. Honestly, it's kind of nice."

A warmth appeared from nowhere, spreading through his chest at the speed of light.

It means nothing, Zeke.

Even if it did, he wasn't in the market for a relationship. Because although he'd said he didn't like pretending, wasn't that kind of what he was doing? He wasn't exactly lying about who he was…far from it. But he had purposely withheld a significant piece of information about his background. But really, why would Shanna need—or even want—to know his life story? They were colleagues. Just like she'd said a moment or two ago.

"Thanks. And, yes, to you introducing me to your mom. I would very much appreciate it. Now are you ready to go see Mr. Landrum?"

"Anytime you are."

With that, they walked down the hallway, chatting about the patient and work stuff rather than things that were of a more personal nature. And that's exactly how he wanted to keep it.

"Okay, so each of you has brought in a picture of what you'd like to carve into your pumpkin, right?"

There were about seven people in the

room, including Zeke, who was again impeccably dressed. Not that he was going to stay that way for long. Not with pumpkin innards squishing through his hands or splattering onto that light blue shirt. She would have a hard time containing her amusement when that happened.

Except wasn't laughing at someone considered cruel?

Yes, it was. And she hoped she wasn't that.

"I've placed a set of tools beside each of your pumpkins and we're going to do a test one. We're not even going to do your planned carving, because I want you guys to do that on your own. But what I am going to teach you is how to use the carving instruments to get a different combination of depths and looks to your pumpkin. You'll have to plan out when and how to use those skills on your own drawings."

"Why did we bring them, then?" The woman who asked the question wasn't being rude. Shanna could see that she was genuinely puzzled.

"I wanted to take a quick look to tell you

whether I think you can easily execute the image on a pumpkin or whether I think you should try for something more simple."

She walked over to Zeke's drawing, which still had the creases from where he'd folded it. The paper had been warm when he'd pulled it free from his pocket and had…

No. No thinking about how it had made her feel. This was about everyone in the room, not just him. She held it up so everyone could see it. "This diagram of a heart might seem complex, but it's really not that involved. It'll make an excellent subject for a pumpkin."

She placed the paper back by the pumpkin she'd provided for a sample carving. Then she went to each of them, looking at their pictures and telling them why the image would work or why it might be difficult to achieve. "Don't let this discourage any of you. I want you to succeed. And part of that includes being honest about how hard something might be to carve. Any questions?"

"Do the carvings need to be related to medicine or anatomy?"

"No, not at all. We've had everything from Cinderella's castle to various animals like whales or dogs, or even people."

She went back to where her own pumpkin was sitting, along with a picture of a jack-o'-lantern. But not the everyday kind. This one had a toothy human grin that she would partially carve, along with eyebrows, and various creases that would happen when someone smiled. "Okay, I assume you all know how to cut open a pumpkin and clean it out. But we're not going to go in through the top like most people do. Instead, we're going to take off the bottom so that we can place our pumpkin over a faux candle. It'll make balancing the pumpkin a little easier than if it were rocking on its normal base. So let's go to work. There are disposable plastic aprons on your chairs if you're worried about your clothes getting dirty."

She wondered if Zeke would utilize the plastic cover.

Since she'd worn old clothes that had splotches of paint on them, she didn't bother with an apron. Instead, she flipped her pumpkin on its side and began cutting a circle out of the thing's bottom, making short work out of it. She then pulled the plug out, a lot of the innards coming with it. "Cutting this way also makes it easier to clean it out."

Glancing up, she saw they were all still sawing at their vegetables, and then heard an oath come from somewhere nearby. When she glanced to the side, she saw that Zeke—sans apron—had sliced all the way through his pumpkin, the knife exiting through the side. She couldn't hold back a laugh that she did her best to disguise as a cough. "We're not trying to create stab wounds in our pumpkins. We just want to take off their bottoms."

Too late, she realized how that sounded and her face turned to an inferno. A couple of people giggled. She wasn't sure if it was because of what Zeke had done or because of what she'd said. And she really didn't care. At this point, she just wanted to get through this.

"Thanks for that clarification." Zeke's reply was dry, but at least he was smiling.

A minute later, he'd removed the base

of his pumpkin and was using a spoon to scoop out the stuff inside. So far, he was still clean as a whistle. The urge to toss a handful of pumpkin guts his way came and went. That would not be professional. At all. And the last thing she wanted anyone to think was that she had some sort of crush on the hospital's newest staff member.

Because she didn't.

But what she had done was offered to introduce him to her mom. That might be considered unprofessional, too, right? Or would it just be seen as being helpful? Because that's all she'd meant by it.

Right?

And then there was her mom. She might jump to the wrong conclusion, too. Except she would be wrong. It wasn't like she was inviting Zeke to be her roommate or anything. Not that she would. Because she couldn't see herself remaining immune to the man for long, if she actually had to see him day in day out. In casual clothes or, worse, running shorts or accidentally seeing him in whatever he wore…or didn't wear to bed at night.

Her face exploded with fire. She turned away for a minute, pretending she was arranging her carving instruments in a specific order. When she glanced around the room, hoping no one had seen her reaction, she saw that most of them had finished cutting open and cleaning out their pumpkins. There were just two more who were still working. "Let's talk tools while we're finishing up."

"We have some punches, some engraving tools, a peeler, some scrapers and various other things that you can feel free to experiment with. You can check them out to use on your actual pumpkins that you enter into the contest, or you can buy your own set. It's completely up to you. Any questions so far?"

One of the techs said, "I could see a good sharp scalpel being useful for this."

"Absolutely. If you have access to some surgical tools, or even a drill with different-sized bits, you can create some amazing designs with just a few simple techniques."

Zeke glanced at her, and she quickly looked away and began talking again. "I'm going to walk you through carving the design I've chosen. Maybe share this with your team and see how you can adapt the different techniques for your design."

Shanna took them step by step through carving the mouth first, answering any questions and going around to help those who needed extra help. "There is no right or wrong way to do this. If you cut deeper into the pumpkin than I do, then your light will be brighter in those areas. If your cuts are more shallow, less light will get through. The idea is to have some areas that go all the way through the pumpkin and others that will help create various areas of light and shadows that will give interest to your depiction."

She could tell Zeke was a surgeon by the way he went about carving his. He paused to plan out each carved groove and execute it with a precision that made her swallow. What other things was he this precise about?

Sex?

The word came and went before she was prepared for it. Oh, Lord, maybe she was developing a crush on the man. Which would be beyond mortifying, since he'd shown zero interest in her. And Shanna didn't have the best track record with men. For some reason, her interest in someone waned almost before it appeared. Most of that was probably residual fear of loss from her dad's unexpected death. One day he'd been in her life, smiling and alive, and the next he'd simply been gone. There'd been no open casket. Nothing other than a metal box with a flag draped across it. The memory of how cold that metal had been when she'd touched it still had the power to sear her emotions.

She shook the thoughts away. But at least they were better than flickering mental images of Zeke slowly undressing in front of her.

Well, hell. She took a wrong angle when carving the space between the teeth and pierced all the way through the pumpkin, much like Zeke had done when cutting open his pumpkin. Her mouth twisted in irritation, but she forced a laugh. "And as you can see, mistakes happen to the best of us.

But don't let it get you down. You can make your mistakes into 'happy little whatevers' like that television artist liked to say."

The class laughed. About a half hour later, her pumpkin was done and a tea light underneath made it come to life. Even her boo-boo wasn't all that noticeable.

She went around from person to person, helping them with trouble spots. When she finally got over to Zeke, she found him, head close to his pumpkin, lines of concentration as he finished up the last little touches on his creation. It was different from hers, but much better than she'd expected it to be from the way he'd talked.

"It looks like you're about done."

"It could be a little more precise." He eyed it with a critical glance that made her smile.

"This isn't brain surgery. Or heart surgery, for that matter. We're allowed creative license with no right or wrong way to do it. Watch. Let's put the light under yours."

She switched on the candle and slid it into the opening under the pumpkin, then set it down. The carving's toothy grin was the thing that stood out the most. She smiled. "It looks kind of like the Cheshire cat from *Alice in Wonderland*."

She drew everyone's attention to the difference between his carving and hers. "See? They're different. But they both draw your eye to particular spots. Just like all of yours will."

Five minutes later, all the pumpkins had their candles turned on and she switched off the light in the room. It made the place magical, just like it always did. She shivered as she looked at all of the carvings. "Good work, you guys. You should be proud of yourselves. Any last questions?"

"How far in advance can we carve our entries?"

"Great question. I wouldn't go more than a couple of days ahead with the way we're doing these carvings. As the pumpkins dry out, parts of them will begin to shrink, changing the look. Anyone else?"

They shook their heads.

"Okay, then consider yourselves officially inducted into the league of pumpkin carvers. Go out and practice or find new designs. Whatever you need to do to get ready for the party. And don't forget your costumes."

"Costumes?" This came from Zeke, and she glanced over at him. "I'm sure I mentioned that one of the other times we talked. It's part of the fun. So yes, if you can, the hospital would appreciate it."

She wasn't sure, but she thought she detected the slightest of eye rolls from the cardiothoracic surgeon. She chose to ignore it.

"If you need to check out your tools, please put your name on the sheet by the door. And the pumpkins and tea lights are yours to take with you."

Almost everyone came over to thank her with smiles, along with some good-natured laughter about how much harder pumpkin carving was than their jobs at the hospital.

Zeke hung back, letting everyone else leave before he came over to her and handed her the tools. She swallowed. God. Had it been so awful that he was going to pull out of the contest?

"I don't understand," she said, glancing down at the case where every tool was back to the pristine, clean condition with which it had started.

"I'll get my own set," he said.

"Does this mean you actually liked carving it?"

"It means I prefer to buy my own set of tools." But this time he smiled, softening the words. "You'll probably never hear me say I actually like carving pumpkins or dressing as outlandish characters. But it's for a good cause, and I'm pretty sure Marcos's parents are bringing him to the party. I don't want to seem like a…"

"Scrooge? Halloween-style?"

That got a low chuckle out of him. "Maybe. Are we still on for meeting your mom?"

"Yep. She knows we're coming and will probably have already done quite a bit of research, knowing her, even though she has no idea what you're looking for yet."

"Honestly, the sooner I can get out of that hotel, the better. Eating takeout every night is getting old. And the walls are a little thinner than I might like."

He didn't say what those walls being a little thinner might be referring to, but all she could picture was a headboard banging late into the night. She gulped, horrified to have pictured herself spread out across a bed with Zeke…

With Zeke nothing. And he was probably talking about a television that was turned up too loud. But when she glanced at him, she got the feeling she'd been right the first time.

"Well, hopefully she can find something you like sooner rather than later."

"Yes, let's hope." He glanced around. "I'll help you get this cleaned up and we can drop my pumpkin off at my office. Then we can go."

She was kind of surprised he hadn't just dumped his carving into the big trash can that she had set up in the room for cleanup. But it made her feel good. That maybe he hadn't completely hated doing it. Although it could be for exactly the reasons he'd mentioned—that he didn't want to disappoint Marcos and his family.

Well, if that was the only reason, she should be glad for it.

And so that's what she was going to try to be. Glad.

Shanna's mom was cordial and super organized. She already had a binder with his name on the front of it and potential properties for him to look through so she could get an idea of his taste.

He smiled over at Shanna. "I see where you get your love of notebooks with dividers."

Grace laughed. "I think we both get that from her father. He was super…organized."

Hadn't Shanna said her dad died when she was ten? He couldn't imagine losing his father at that age. Couldn't imagine losing him now, honestly. And it was happening. Little by little, and there was nothing Zeke could do to stop it. When he glanced over at Shanna, she was staring at her mom as if looking for something.

Grace sent her a quick smile and said, "I'll be back in a minute."

He sat on a large gray sectional sofa, binder opened to a listing of a small bungalow, while Shanna's mom left the room. With her dark hair and brown eyes, she looked much like her daughter, who was currently sitting on the far end of the sofa.

He turned his concentration back to the listings and flipped to the next page.

Hell, there were more houses available than he'd expected. Honestly, probably any of them would do, but he wanted Grace's take on areas within a reasonable distance from the hospital. He didn't really want to be a half hour away, stuck in bumper-to-bumper traffic during his commute, if he could help it. Maybe he'd gotten spoiled by how close he was now. But staying in a hotel forever wasn't the best choice, either.

Shanna had been pretty quiet. Maybe she was just tired. Or maybe she was regretting bringing him to meet his mother, despite her earlier words. Well, he wouldn't stay any longer than necessary.

That pumpkin-carving class had been something else. Watching Shanna flit from person to person, helping them figure out difficult areas, was a revelation. No wonder she seemed to be so good at her job. She was able to multitask in a way that surprised him. He tended to be laser focused during surgery and found that things that broke his concentration were annoying. He tended to like quiet in his surgical suite. He knew of medics in the army who liked to have music blaring as they patched up wounds both big and small, but he preferred a quiet scene with minimal chitchat. Just the stuff that needed saying. He'd only had a couple of surgeries at the hospital so far, Matthew Landrum's and two that had come through the ER. He was still getting used to the way things were run at Everly, but so far he'd been pleased at the level of skill he'd found at the hospital.

"Find something?" Shanna's voice interrupted his thoughts and he turned to glance at her, realizing he'd stopped turning pages again.

He glanced down and saw that it was a two-bedroom, one-bath fixer-upper. No, that probably wasn't the best idea for someone who ran on coffee and adrenaline. "No. I just have no idea what I'm even looking for."

She scooted closer and glanced down at the listing. "That's quite a way from the hospital. You'd have to cross the Sunshine Skyway every day on your way to work."

"That's the big bridge?"

"Yep. Crossing it daily is something I would consider a nightmare. But then I'm not a huge fan of heights and avoid that bridge whenever possible."

He smiled. "I didn't think anything scared you."

She shrugged, her glance flickering to the doorway her mom had gone through. "You'd be surprised."

She didn't elaborate on the other things that frightened her and he didn't ask.

"So where do you suggest I look for places?"

She moved even closer. "May I?" She nodded to the book.

"Of course."

Her fingers touched his as she reached for the plastic page protectors her mom had slid each listing into. He moved his hand, trying to make it seem more casual than it was. Her touch had gone through him like an electric shock and the urge to feel it again made a ball of tension coil inside him, just like when they'd drank coffee together and she'd covered his hand with hers.

He'd been shocked by his response then. Evidently that hadn't changed between that day and this one.

She flipped the page to the beginning. "If I know my mom, she probably put these in some kind of specific order, the closest properties to the hospital toward the beginning of the binder. Ah, yes. See here? This particular apartment complex is just a block away from work. But if I remember right, these are small units, maybe not much bigger than the hotel room you're currently in."

"I don't need much. But I would like something in a quiet place. Being woken up in the middle of the night isn't my favorite way to spend an evening."

Her face turned a pink shade that he found more attractive than he should have. "I can imagine. Living in any kind of hotel room wouldn't be my idea of fun."

"It's not. Which is why I'd like to find something else pretty quick."

The rhythmic thumping against the wall in the room next to his had happened on a couple of nights and had made him grit his teeth, trying not to imagine what was taking place.

She smiled, the move crinkling the skin near her eyes in a way that was damn attractive. She'd never mentioned a significant other, but then why would she have? For some reason, though, he didn't think she was involved with anyone. She wasn't checking her phone constantly the way he'd seen some of the other staff members doing.

Her attention went back to the binder as she flipped another page. "Are you looking for an apartment, or a house?"

Really, he'd thought either one would be

fine, but thinking about the upkeep involved in having a yard… Maybe an apartment or condo would be better. This place hadn't been all that far from the hospital. It had taken maybe fifteen minutes to get here. "Are there any units in this complex in that binder?"

"This complex?" A look of alarm crossed her expression before she wiped it away.

"What? Do you live here as well as your mom?" Maybe she didn't want him living nearby. But why? Was she afraid he was going to hit on her?

Hell, hadn't he just wondered if she was involved with anyone? He hoped he wasn't sending off some kind of stalker vibes. But then again, she wouldn't have suggested he talk to her mom if she was genuinely worried about it, right?

She shook her head. "No. Actually, I live in the house I grew up in after my father… Well, for a lot of my school years."

After her dad had died? Her demeanor right now didn't invite questions, though, and he couldn't blame her. He rarely mentioned his dad's diagnosis. But when he'd gone into the reserves, he'd wanted a duty station that was close enough to his parents that he could make it over there in a few hours by car. He'd done his research and there were some great facilities that specialized in memory care. Now all he had to do was get his mom to agree to move.

It was strange to see the man who'd been such a strong, powerful force in his life whittled down to a shell of his former self. His mom had been a bastion of strength, though, much like Shanna's mom seemed to be. Much like Shanna herself seemed to be.

Grace came back into the room, carrying a wooden tray with an elaborate array of meat, cheeses and small slices of crusty bread spread over it.

"You didn't have to do that. I'm already asking a big enough favor."

"It's nothing. And it's fun to dip my toes back into the housing market."

Dipping her toes? From the number of pages in the binder in front of him, it seemed more than just that. She probably did like sorting through properties. "Have you been a Realtor long?"

"About twenty-five years. I had started taking courses, and then when Jack was killed, it made finishing a necessity."

"Jack?"

"My late husband. Shanna's dad."

CHAPTER FIVE

GOD, WHY HAD her mom had to mention her dad's death? She made herself as small as possible when Zeke's gaze swung to her.

"You mentioned your dad died when you were a kid. I'm sorry. I should have realized."

"It happened a long time ago."

Grace spoke up. "Jack is the reason Shanna likes Halloween so much. They used to carve pumpkins together. They won quite a few ribbons."

Why had she ever thought bringing Zeke here was a good idea? Her mom was an open book, rarely feeling the need to hide anything from those she met. No matter how uncomfortable it might make her daughter.

"That explains a lot," Zeke said.

Did it? He had no idea what it was like to lose a parent for a reason that was so stupid that it boggled the mind. A pipe bomb, of all things. They'd cleared the area of IEDs, only to have a bomb hidden in supplies they had ordered. If not for her dad, a lot of men would have died. Instead, it had been just her dad.

Her chin went up and she decided to challenge Zeke's words, although she wasn't entirely sure why. "Exactly what does it explain?"

"Why you took it on yourself to create a Halloween event at the hospital."

Her ire deflated almost as quickly as it had risen up. Because he was exactly right. Halloween was a way she could keep her dad's memory fresh and vibrant in her head. How often had she thought about how her dad would appreciate some new tool or carving technique? He would have been a much better teacher than she was at classes like the one she'd held earlier today.

But he wasn't here. And while her mom still loved going to parades that honored the armed forces, Shanna wasn't quite as quick to stand there and wave a flag. While she understood the need to help keep world peace, how many fathers had died—just like hers had—trying to attain what seemed like an impossible goal?

Shanna had decided long ago that she wouldn't date a military man, just because it would always be in the back of her mind that the unthinkable actually did happen. Probably more often than she realized.

But she wouldn't tell her mom any of that. She was proud of her husband. Proud of his unwavering commitment. Proud of the way he'd loved her and his daughter with the same unwavering devotion.

It was on the tip of her tongue to ask about his own parents, but it didn't feel right prying into his personal life. If she hadn't liked her mom laying it all out there, Zeke probably wouldn't appreciate a direct question, either.

Her mom must have sensed that things had become awkward, because she handed Zeke a plate and urged him to have some of the items on the charcuterie tray. It was one of her mom's favorite things to make.

And she was good at it. Maybe because she had one at most open houses that she'd held. They had always been such a huge hit.

Zeke selected a few items, placing them on the small plate in front of him. When her mom gave her a pointed look, she took a plate and did the same, although she'd never really felt less like eating. For one thing, she was worried about her mom. The same way she always worried about her whenever she talked about her husband's death. Like Shanna, she was a master at hiding her emotions. It was another reason she avoided talking about her dad. She never wanted her mom to slide down into another pit of despair.

"So I was asking Shanna if there are any units available in this complex."

Ugh. Of course he hadn't forgotten the question. And honestly the condo community was big enough that even if he bought one of them, they wouldn't necessarily run into each other every time she came to visit her mom. So what was the problem with him living here?

Maybe it was just knowing that he *was* there, even if she never saw him in the flesh.

Her mom sat on the other side of Zeke and flipped through several pages. "Actually, there are three units available. Two two-bedrooms and a three-bedroom."

"Two bedrooms would be plenty. I don't entertain much at all."

He didn't? For some reason, she'd gotten the idea he could have any woman he wanted. And maybe he could. Maybe he just chose not to do his "socializing" at home. Or maybe his surgeries were so stressful that he chose a quieter life when he was in his own space. She couldn't blame him. Her own social calendar wasn't exactly filled to the brim, except during Halloween. Once the hospital party was over, she'd go back to her own quiet corner of the world.

"Bayfront Condos has a pretty big footprint, but it's a nice quiet area." She smiled. "If you tend to throw wild parties, you might run into a bit of trouble with the homeowners' association."

She'd heard some of those homeowners' associations could be pretty nitpicky with what they allowed or didn't allow within the community. But HOAs definitely had their place. They were probably the reason there were no wild parties going on late into the night.

"No wild parties. In all honesty, I probably wouldn't be here all that much. When I have a few days off, I'd run up to see my folks in Jacksonville."

So his parents were both still alive. Did he realize how lucky he was?

Probably. And since he liked to go see them as often as possible, they must have a pretty good relationship.

She was happy for him. But it also removed some of her reticence about him possibly living in her mom's condo association. After all, if what he said was true, he really wouldn't be there a lot.

"Would it be possible to see one of the units?"

"Sure. I have the code for the lockboxes. And the units are all empty at the moment, so we wouldn't have to worry about notifying the owners. So you said two-bedroom, right?"

"Yes."

Grace scooped up a slice of sausage, spreading what looked like mustard from a little pot on the piece of meat before popping it in her mouth. "Shanna, do you want to come?"

What was she going to say? No? That she would just hang around her mom's condo and wait for them to come back? That would seem churlish somehow. So she stood to her feet. "Sure. I wouldn't mind seeing the units, either."

"We'll take my car. It's not that they're far, but Florida's downpours sometimes come out of nowhere."

Zeke smiled, and she found herself staring for some reason. The curving of his lips carved a divot in his left cheek that was attractive in a way she couldn't explain. She'd seen plenty of dimples before, but this was more than that. It was more of a craggy line that her fingers itched to explore.

Not that she would ever get the chance. Nor did she want that chance. Right?

"Sun showers were what we called them," he said.

"We do as well. The sun can be shining, even as the rain is pounding on the sidewalks across the city."

"Any other properties that strike your fancy that you want to go see?"

"I haven't had a chance to look at all of them. Is there any way I can take that binder back to the hotel with me and look at it in more depth?"

"Of course. It's what I meant for you to do with it."

"Thank you for taking the time to put it together. I know it must have taken hours."

She smiled. "It's as much my passion as Halloween is my daughter's."

"I can certainly appreciate that."

Zeke's passion was probably his work, from what she'd seen. He saved lives and helped his patients have more quality years doing what they enjoyed. Like Mr. Landrum.

And even Marcos, even though the boy wasn't specifically Zeke's patient. But he could have done what other doctors had done. Sent the boy and his family home with antibiotics to fight an infection that wasn't at the heart of his problems. That cycle had probably happened more than once.

They piled in her mom's SUV and drove less than five minutes to another section of the condominium. Like the section her mom lived in, this area had pristine white buildings surrounded by lush green and floral landscaping. Shanna couldn't imagine living anywhere else. Tampa was beautiful with its white Gulf beaches and ocean breezes.

"It's in this unit on the ground floor. The other two-bedroom is on the third floor, depending on which you'd prefer."

"Are they exactly alike other than what floor they're on?"

"No, they're decorated completely different. One has a beach cottage vibe, while this one is ultra-modern. Obviously, you can have it redone according to your own taste. I'll take you to see the other one after this. It's on the far side of the property."

Walking up to the door of an end unit, Zeke nodded. "I like that it's on the end."

"Yes, those units don't come up for sale very often." She punched a code on the lockbox and it snapped open, letting her retrieve a key to the unit, which she used to open the door.

Swinging it wide, she motioned for Zeke and Shanna to go in ahead of her. Shanna was surprised by how different this place was from her mom's cozy-looking decor. Ultra-modern was right, from the chrome and leather furniture, down to the white marble flooring, which was devoid of a rug or anything that might soften the space. The dining room table was an expanse of glass with chunky chrome legs and accompanying white upholstered chairs.

She frowned. It was too cold. Too stark for her taste. But maybe that's what Zeke liked.

He wandered around the unit, not saying much, and her mom didn't push him for an opinion, instead letting him explore the unit at his leisure. It's what made her such a good Realtor.

"How many square feet is this unit?"

Her mom didn't consult her listing, just said, "Eleven hundred. The second unit we'll see has the same basic layout although it has a master suite with a bathroom, whereas this one doesn't."

"I see."

They followed him to the hallway, which had three doors along it. All closed.

He opened the first one and revealed a smallish bedroom that was in keeping with the theme. It boasted a silver, shiny tubular headboard, white bedspread and white plush carpeting. "Is this the master?"

"No, this is the guest room. The master bedroom is the last door on the left."

The bathroom was also all shiny furnishings and fixtures that bounced light onto every possible surface. She wrinkled her nose, only to have her mom frown at her.

Okay, she knew she wasn't supposed to have an opinion. After all, she wasn't going to be sharing this space with him. Or any other space for that matter. But somehow she'd be disappointed if this was the place he chose.

Guys were supposed to like modern minimalist, weren't they?

"Do the furnishings come with the unit?" he asked.

"They do. They're included in the price."

"I see."

He opened the door to the last room and Shanna almost laughed. While it was modern as well, it had some sort of faux animal hide tossed diagonally across the bed. It looked like…giraffe? But it seemed so impractical as to be almost ludicrous.

"Okay, I think I've seen all there is. Do you have time to run to the other unit?"

"I do."

Locking the place back up, Shanna was glad to be back out where there were at least splashes of color from the landscaping. All that white would drive her batty in no time flat. She'd have to get rid of most of the furniture in order to live there.

Whether Zeke loved it or hated it was impossible to tell. The man would make a great poker player, his face giving nothing away.

When they got to the next unit, they had to walk up two flights of stairs and the unit wasn't on the end like the other one had been. But since there were only three floors, there would be no one above his. The second her mom opened the door, Shanna fell in love. She was right when she said it was decorated like a beach cottage. But while she normally thought of those as filled with soft blue colors and muted flowers, this wasn't overly feminine. This place also had its share of glass surfaces, including the round dining room table, but it was softer. The dining room chairs were made of light whitewashed wood and there was a gas fireplace, which struck her as humorous in this part of Florida. But there were chilly days here for sure, and the idea of a glass of wine while watching the flames dance held an appeal that the other unit hadn't offered.

Large, bleached pieces of coral were artfully placed on flat surfaces, and there was a large round clock over the fireplace. She was glad there wasn't a television perched there, although it probably would have been convenient to have one in that spot.

She glanced at Zeke, whose face was just as impassive as it had been in the other unit. The appliances in the galley kitchen were high-end and, while they were stainless, it still didn't have a cold feel. Maybe because of the tiles of the backsplash, which looked like they'd had some sort of paint technique applied to give them a softer appearance. She reached out to touch it, expecting it to be delicate or easily scratched, but it wasn't. It felt almost like concrete.

"It's called German smear. It's a technique that's popular in homes today," her mom explained.

"Is it concrete?"

Her mom nodded. "It's a mortar that's kind of smeared on to create a textured surface. It's where the name of the technique comes from."

"I'm surprised by how nice it looks in here."

Zeke glanced at her. "So you like this, do you?"

She bit her lip, knowing she'd probably broken one of her mom's unspoken rules, but it was too late to take it back. "I really do." In her own best interest and so as not to earn herself a lecture later on, she kept the rest of her opinion to herself as Zeke walked from room to room.

The master bedroom boasted the same

whitewashed beachy-looking furniture, the low chunky posters of the bed seeming to be in keeping with the rest of the unit. And no giraffe hide tossed across this bed. Instead there was a white bedspread, whose nubby textured pattern reminded her of sand somehow. And when she followed him through to the bathroom, she stopped in her tracks. This was a study in muted luxury. A soaking tub that stood on the far wall was what you saw when you first entered the space. A white distressed board was placed across the span of the tub, and on it was a dark brown candle that gave the impression of tree bark. Again, not too feminine. The shower had a sprayer on either side of the space, making it obvious it would hold two people easily.

She did her best not to picture Zeke in that space with her, but it was a struggle. One she was losing. She finally backed out of the room, waiting in the bedroom, instead. That didn't help. Because she could picture some nameless couple exiting the bathroom, soaking wet and falling onto the luxurious bedding.

Nameless couple?

Not so much, because the couple wasn't nameless at all. She was picturing her and Zeke. Again.

What the hell was wrong with her? She'd had a couple of relationships in the past, but they always fizzled out pretty quickly. And she'd never had fantasies like these. With her mother standing nearby, of all things.

Worse was that she might be picturing herself twined together with the cardiac surgeon, but there was no evidence that he was doing the same with her. No surreptitious glances. No hooded looks.

Just a man who was looking for an apartment rather than a partner.

And she wasn't in search of a partner, either. She was happy the way she was. She had a career she loved, friends that she went out and had fun with on a regular basis. She didn't need a man to make her life complete.

So what was that gnawing sensation in her belly when she remembered the way those women had looked him over in the coffee shop the other day?

Well, if it was any consolation, he hadn't

even noticed them. At least not that she was aware of. Ha! If she'd been one of those women, she'd have gotten the same oblivious reaction from him, more than likely.

They came out of the bathroom and Zeke's gaze slid over her before shifting to the bed. Her insides turned hot. It had to be a coincidence. She'd simply been in his line of sight, that was all. But even so, the way it had made her feel sent off warning bells inside her. Because what if he did notice her at some point? What if he was willing to share his bed with her? Would she go along with it?

Evidently that was a no-brainer judging from her reaction.

Zeke turned to her mom. "Does this also include the furnishings? Everything we see?"

The way he said it intensified the heat inside her as if he were referring to her. He wasn't. And she had better scrub that thought from her head, before it burrowed deep and threatened to taunt her late into the night.

"It does. Right down to the linens and cutlery."

"Can I see that listing again?"

She handed him the binder and watched as he studied the specs and probably mulled over the price, whether it was in line with what he was willing to pay.

"I like this one, actually. I think I'd like to put an offer in on it."

Yes! The internal fist bump she gave herself was way out of line. Especially with her initial dismay that he might choose a condo in this particular complex. And her mom would have given her "what for" if she could read her thoughts. But despite all of that, something inside her was stoked that he would choose this place over that cold, emotionless unit they'd just come from. This place had emotion. And despite the cool whitewashed color palette, there was a heat that ran just below the surface.

Or maybe she was getting herself confused with the condo.

But the image of his glance going to her before sliding across that bed would be one that she was going to have a hard time banishing, no matter if he'd been picturing her sprawled out on that bed or not. Because she could do enough picturing for the both of them.

And right now, she was wishing she hadn't come with them. Wished she had simply introduced him to her mom and then driven herself home. She didn't want to know what his future place was going to look like. And she certainly didn't want to picture him naked in that shower, being pummeled by hot streams of water, which would pour down his hair and sluice down his chest before finding other areas in which to play.

Oh, God, this had been such a huge mistake. Was it wrong to hope that the contract didn't go through? And that he would find some other place to live? A place she couldn't actually picture in her mind?

"Are you sure you don't want to look any further?" Her mom was the consummate professional. She didn't want him to look back and have buyer's remorse later on.

His glance went to her again before jerking away. "I think I've looked far enough. I know what I want."

He knew what he wanted? Okay, maybe she wasn't imagining it. Surely there'd been some hint of awareness in those impossibly blue eyes.

But even if there were, it didn't mean that either one of them had to act on it. In fact, that could prove to be a disaster since they worked together professionally. She'd seen some pretty ugly breakups after hospital romances. The last thing she wanted were the pitying glances she'd given others who'd been through exactly that.

It did make her feel better, though, that she might not be as crazy as she'd thought.

And she was still weirdly happy that he'd liked the beachy condo rather than the first one.

"Okay, let's go back to my place and we'll write it up."

This was probably where she should make her exit. "Well, I'll head home and let you two talk business."

"Nonsense," her mom said. "We should

go out and celebrate. That is if Zeke is okay doing that."

"Actually, that sounds good." He looked at Shanna again. "Thanks for suggesting your mom. This process was a lot more painless than I expected it to be."

"You've never bought a house before?"

"Nope. Never. But there's a first time for everything, right?"

"Absolutely," her mom said. "And I can't imagine a better place than the one you picked out. It was honestly my favorite out of all the ones in that binder, although my taste doesn't always line up with someone else's, so I try not to do much in the way of trying to influence my clients."

"And I appreciate that. I really do."

They got back to Grace's place and wrote up a contract. He'd been glad to get out of the place, because he'd noticed Shanna's eyes light up when she'd seen that shower, and it had sent all kinds of crazy thoughts spinning through his head. And if he had read her right, she'd had the same kinds of ideas. And watching color infuse her face when his gaze had landed on the bed had given him a sense of satisfaction that was far too appealing. Far too dangerous.

And he'd actually been glad her mom was there, because it meant he couldn't act on any of those impulses. It had probably saved him a lot of grief in the long run. A brief romp in the bedroom was one thing, but there was something about Shanna that seemed to hint that she wasn't one to blithely have one-night stands. He wasn't sure how he knew that, but it was there in the way she didn't openly try to figure out if the attraction was mutual and then let him know she was there for the asking.

Which meant he needed to tread a lot more carefully around her. Needed to watch his step and make sure he didn't do something that might hurt her without meaning to. He hadn't wanted to hurt Kristen, and he didn't think he had. She'd been the one who'd wanted to exit the relationship once she realized he wasn't going to leave the military for her. Leaving the service was something that needed to happen on his own terms. When the timing felt right. And it hadn't back then. And it still didn't. It was why he'd opted to go into the reserves once his required time on active duty had ended. Maybe it was as a tribute to his dad. He wasn't quite sure. He just knew that right now staying in felt like the right thing to do.

But changing from active duty to reserves also meant that base housing was no longer available for him to use like it had been before. So buying his own housing was new to him. He could certainly see how it would have its own benefits in that he would be investing in something that could increase in value.

"So how soon before I hear something?"

"We'll probably hear back on whether the offer was accepted pretty quickly. In the meantime, we need to get you preapproved for a mortgage, but I can help you do that. It'll also give you a ballpark figure of price ranges, in case this particular unit doesn't work out."

The problem was, he really wanted it to. His credit rating was excellent and doing some quick figuring in his head, he should be able to afford the payments on the condo with no problems.

Grace signed off on the contract and Zeke also signed where she'd indicated. "I'll go ahead and send this over to the listing Realtor and go from there. Be right back. You and Shanna decide where you want to eat."

The second she left the room, he went over to one of the windows and looked out onto the property. The lawns were well manicured and tastefully landscaped. In the distance he could see some kind of pond with a misty spray erupting from the middle of it. Florida had a lot of these that, while beautiful, also helped deal with the runoff that came with inches and inches of rain per year. They also attracted gators. The funny thing was, most people who weren't from Florida feared the creatures. But for the most part they weren't aggressive unless they'd lost their fear of humans, even though they were a danger to small pets that ventured too close to the edge of those areas.

He glanced at her. "Do you get many gators in Tampa?"

"Our fair share. Although you probably got some, too, when you lived in the Panhandle, even though winters can be colder. The Okefenokee Swamp in Georgia has quite a few, even."

"They do. I've canoed the trail there many times."

She smiled at him. "Me, too, actually. It was always a popular destination spot when I was in college."

"So you preferred canoeing to the night life?"

"After a busy day at school, the last thing I wanted to do was go out and party. There were certainly those who did, but the group I hung out with was pretty boring."

"You? Boring? Not a chance."

Surprisingly she smiled at that. "I don't know whether to take that as a compliment or a cut."

"A compliment for sure. I was pretty boring myself." Except for the times when duty had called on him to treat wounded soldiers in less-than-ideal circumstances. But those were his memories. Memories that he'd struggled with. He didn't need to push them off on her.

"So if I agree with you, will you get mad?"

"You think I'm boring?" He sat up a little straighter.

She laughed. "How can anyone who doesn't embrace all that Halloween has to offer be anything but boring?"

"I liked carving that pumpkin. Does that earn me any brownie points?"

A flicker of surprise crossed her face. "You did? I thought you were just being polite."

One thing he wasn't going to say was that part of the reason he liked it was because she'd made it interesting. By her body language. By the way her tongue peeked out of the side of her mouth when she was concentrating on a particularly intricate part of carving her pumpkin. The way she was able to laugh at herself when she'd accidentally punched a hole through the pumpkin when doing the teeth.

"That surprises me. Doesn't my expression give away my every emotion?" His lips canted sideways when her face transformed from shocked confusion to one of irony.

"Very funny. I remember thinking that you'd make a great poker player with how little your face moves. You'd make a great spokesman for Botox."

"Botox. I think that's a slight exaggeration."

Her head tilted. "Maybe. You do have slight lines right here." She touched the corner of his eyes, the sensation of her fingertips sliding across that area sending a shudder through him.

Right then her mom walked back into the room and Shanna jerked her hand away so fast it probably gave her whiplash. Well, if his expression was stony, hers was the opposite. She looked mortified and embarrassed.

Grace looked from one to the other, but before she could draw the wrong conclusions, he said, "I had a spot of dirt on my face. She was brushing it away."

Shanna's shoulders actually sagged in relief. He really should warn her that her body language gave most of her thoughts and emotions away.

Like when she'd looked at that shower and made him see it through her eyes.

"Okay, are we ready to go eat?" Grace asked.

Yes. More than ready. The sooner he got out of this condo and pressed reset on this crazy day, the better. Then tomorrow, everything could go back to normal.

At least he hoped it could. Because if not, he was in big trouble. A kind of trouble that could creep up like a gator and bite him in the ass when he least expected it. The key was to make sure he didn't let it.

CHAPTER SIX

"SORRY, GUYS, CAN I catch up with you at the restaurant? The listing agent wants some more information. Zeke, are you willing to go up to the listing price if needed?"

Shanna stood there shell-shocked. She knew her mom well enough to know she was telling the truth. There was no match-making involved here, but still...

"I'm willing to go ten thousand over the listing price, if there are other people trying to get it."

"Great, that's all I needed to know. Let me know where you wind up and I'll meet you there as soon as I can."

She looked at Zeke. "Don't feel obligated to go if you don't want to."

"I'd like to find out if I'm in the running

for the unit or not. Unless you don't want to go."

Great. Now if she said no, her mom was sure to look at her a little more closely and wonder what was going on. "I'm fine with it, just didn't want you to feel pushed into something you don't want to do."

Like she did right now? It wasn't that she didn't want to go. She did. And she wasn't sure why. Maybe she was better off not knowing, though. Surely it had nothing to do with getting a peek inside the man's head as far as his taste in decor went. Surely sitting with him in a restaurant without her mom was better than having her analyzing everything either of them said or did.

Although why would her mom do that? Unless Shanna gave her reason to. And if she knew her mom, she would probably become so immersed in the game of buying and selling that she might not make dinner at all.

Leaving just the two of them. Her and Zeke. And a roomful of other patrons. Her mouth twisted. It wasn't like they'd be at a private table in a secret room in the restaurant. Something that only happened in the movies.

"I don't feel pushed."

Shanna had to scramble to figure out what he was talking about. God. He was simply responding to her last statement.

She nodded as if she wasn't totally discombobulated. "Do you like Cuban food? There's a place on the bay that is authentic. The owner is my second cousin, actually."

Her mom nodded. "You'll love La Terrazza. I'll call if there's a problem on this end. In the meantime, go and enjoy yourselves."

At least with Tereza there, there could be no footsies under the table. Not that there would be. Why on earth had she offered to introduce him to her mother? It would have been better off to leave their relationship where it was. Which was exactly nowhere. He could have found his own Realtor and Shanna wouldn't now be introducing him to yet another member of her family.

Suddenly eating at her cousin's place seemed like a very bad idea.

"Why don't we take my vehicle, and you can ride back with your mom?"

Okay, maybe this wouldn't be such a disaster after all. She wouldn't be forced to play the awkward games of being dropped off at the condo.

"That sounds like a plan."

Grace paused with her thumb poised over a button on her phone. "Give Tereza a big hug from me." Then she held the phone up to her ear. A second later she was headed for the kitchen, the binder in her hand as she read something from the listing.

Her mom was super nice in person, but as a Realtor she was nothing if not efficient. And a little bit ruthless. It was rare for her to lose a sale once she had her mind set on it. And it sounded like she'd just shifted into that persona. Lord help whoever that listing Realtor was.

"I guess that's our cue to head out," Zeke said.

His car wasn't what she pictured a high-powered surgeon to drive. It was an SUV, but not the newest model. Did she really judge people like that?

Lord, she hoped not. Her own ride was a five-year-old model, but it was clean and purred like a kitten. It was also a lot lower to the ground than his.

She stepped onto the running board and into the vehicle, letting him slam the door behind her. Once he got in, he looked at her. "Top up...or down?"

Her eyes got wide. "What?"

"The top to the car." His mouth twisted. "I guess that could have been construed as something else entirely."

"Obviously I knew you didn't mean my top." Except that is what she'd thought for just a second, before she realized she was being ridiculous.

"So my question remains. Car top up or down?"

"Down, please. It's warm out today and it's not often I ride in a convertible." She reached into her purse and pulled out a clip for her hair. The last thing she needed was for it to be tangled in one huge knot when they reached La Terrazza.

"Down it is."

He started the car and pushed a button

and the roof accordioned onto itself, folding down in stages until it disappeared into the frame of the car. Once they moved out of the parking lot, the warm air sifted past her skin and she raised her face to the sun and let the currents flow over her. It revived her, much as the sea breezes had the power to do when she sat in the soft powdery sands of the Gulf and listened to the seabirds as they went by.

"Have you ever seen the sunset over the Gulf?"

"Only from the Panhandle, but I assume it's even more magnificent sitting on a beach that faces west."

"You need to see it. So very gorgeous."

He glanced at his smartwatch. "I would say we could cross the bridge into Clearwater before dinner, but we still have an hour and a half until sunset, and if your mom is planning on meeting us at the restaurant…"

"I know." She sighed, trying not to make it sound as wistful as it felt. It had been quite a while since she'd actually made time to sit on the beach. It was another of the things she'd loved to do with her dad…

walk along the shoreline and watch for dolphins that liked to play along the coast. It had been more than twenty years since his death. And while his memory would never die, there were times when she had trouble bringing his face into focus, times when she couldn't remember how his shirts smelled as she nestled against his chest and listened to his stories.

Zeke looked over at her. "Tell you what. If we can't do it tonight, you'll have to take me to your favorite spot sometime, so I know where to go to see it."

Just as they pulled into the parking lot of La Terrazza, her cell phone buzzed in her purse. When she pulled it out, she saw it was her mom. "Hi, Mom. Did you get your calls made?"

"I did, but I'm not going to make it to dinner. A friend called and she needs me to come over and look at some discoloration on her wall. But tell Zeke that the owner accepted his offer and will pay closing costs. We did have to go up to list price but didn't have to go over it. He'll need to come in and get his financial stuff together for the mortgage company."

"That's great news." She held her hand over the speaker. "Mom said the owner accepted the offer at list price and they'll pay for closing costs."

"Tell her thank you, for me."

"He says thanks."

Her mom gave a few more details and then said goodbye. She had to go look at discoloration on a friend's wall? That sounded fishy to her, but no way was she going to let Zeke know of her suspicions. "The bad news is she's not going to be able to make dinner. She's off to help a friend who has an issue with her house."

"Okay." He paused a second or two. "So what would you rather do? Go to dinner? Or head to Clearwater?"

"Clearwater, unless you're starving."

"With that meat and cheese tray your mom had, I have to admit, I'm not super hungry."

"Me, either." She shot him a look. "Are you sure you wouldn't rather just drop me off at my mom's and head home, since you don't have to fill out any more paperwork on your future house? Congratulations, by the way."

"Thanks. And you forget, I have no home right now. Just a hotel room that leaves a little to be desired as far as peace and quiet goes."

"It'll take about forty minutes to get to Clearwater Beach, but it's worth it, and we'll hit it just before sunset. If you're sure you want to go."

He nodded. "I'm sure."

Shanna explained that Clearwater Beach was actually a barrier island, connected to the mainland through a long causeway. Since he grew up on the east coast of Florida rather than the west, it was like entering a different world. There were no large waves like they had in the Jacksonville/Saint Augustine area. Just white sand and calm clear waters.

And he was used to going to the beach to see the sun rise rather than to watch it set. It was one of the funny things about Florida. Its long and relatively narrow shape made it possible to watch the sun come up over the water on one side and then drive across the state to the other side where you could watch it set over a different body of water.

The trip over had been nice. A little too nice. He'd enjoyed her touristy chatter about the things that the west coast had to offer, and he'd also enjoyed watching her twist her hair back up into its comb when too many strands escaped. They played around her neck and face, the silky locks looking far too inviting.

Yes. He was glad she'd wanted the top down. It was probably the only time he'd ever see her so...*disheveled*, although that wasn't really the word he was looking for.

He wracked his brain for another one that would better fit what she looked like from where he sat.

Sexy. Yes, the woman looked sexy as hell with the top of her scrubs ruffling in the stiff breeze, the slightly V-neck offering peekaboo glances at the skin just below its border. Not that he could take his eyes off the road long enough to ogle. And not that he would. But his imagination was working overtime at filling in some very tantalizing blanks.

He got to the end of the causeway and when they were beachside, he stopped, pulling off the road and looking at her. No more fluttering. No more peeks. But, damn, he was glad, because things were starting to get a little more uncomfortable with every mile they traveled. "Which way from here?"

"Let's turn right and go past Pier 60 and sit on the beach. The pier is neat, but it's bound to be crowded right now."

"So that's the pier?"

"That's it. A fishing and tourist mecca. And a great place to catch the sunset...if you're a fan of crowds. And I don't advise coming out here during spring break."

That made him laugh. "Noted."

He glanced to the left. Pier 60 was a long dock that hung out over the Gulf. And true to what Shanna said, there were people crowding the rail on its west side. It had what looked like shelters along its stretch and then in the middle of it there was an actual building. Scattered on the sand surrounding the area were vendors selling everything from truck food to umbrellas. "What is that structure on the pier?"

"It's a bait store and shop. Let's drive down a ways. It'll be easier to park and the crowds won't be so terrible."

They traveled until they found a public parking area and Zeke pushed a button to raise the top. She glanced at him and laughed. "Well, it's not super obvious we work at a hospital, is it?"

They both still had their lanyards around their necks, and while he was in jeans and a shirt, Shanna was in dark blue scrubs with pictures of elephants all over them. He smiled. "I think your getup is a little more obvious than mine." He dropped his lanyard into a compartment in his vehicle. "Do you want to leave yours inside as well?"

"Yep." She pulled it over her head and slid it into her purse. "If you're going to lock the car, I won't bother bringing anything with me."

"I am."

They climbed out of the vehicle, and he locked the door.

Then they were walking toward the

beach. Shanna kicked off her rubber clogs and stuffed her socks inside them, opting to carry them rather than keep them on her feet. She had glittery pink polish on her toenails that shimmered in the sun. Somehow it fit her to a T.

They stepped onto the beach, and he soon saw that it wasn't as hard-packed as some of the beaches on the other coast. He ended up taking off his own shoes to make walking in the sand a little easier.

"I was wondering if you were going to tough it out."

"I figured I'd have to take them off sooner or later. But remind me to take my cues from those around me."

Not one person still had their shoes on. It made him smile. It had been a while since he'd actually stood barefooted on a beach. Maybe not since Kristen, although she wasn't much of a beachgoer. They'd visited a nearby beach in Panama City probably twice during their relationship.

His mouth twisted. Looking back, they'd had more arguments than good times. Especially in the last year of their relationship.

But, still, to come home to an empty apartment had been a jolt he'd never quite gotten over. Maybe because he knew that someday he would visit his mom and have to face an empty bed where his dad would have slept.

Something cramped inside him and he forced it to release its grip. That day was not now. His dad was still with them, even if he was slipping away little by little.

He'd been to see them before moving to Tampa, but the urge to make the four-hour drive was strong. Maybe with this next trip, he could broach the subject of moving them to the area. There was even that ground-floor condo he'd looked at today, and he was sure there were others like it in different parts of the city.

But for now he would focus on what was here in front of him. The beach. The sun. And the sand. His dad would have liked the pier and the fishing. If they moved in time, maybe he could still bring him out here and help him do some of the things he'd liked the most.

She walked a little farther down the beach and then found an area away from people and dropped onto the sand, giving no thought to the lack of a towel. "Mmm...it's still so warm."

He blinked before she answered his mental question. "The beach. It's still warm from the sun."

She patted the sand next to her. "Try it and see."

He settled onto the beach and closed his eyes. She was right. The beach held on to the heat from the sun, even though that orb was hanging a little lower in the sky than it had been fifteen minutes ago. He was glad they'd come here rather than the restaurant. Glad that Grace hadn't been able to come, although he felt a twinge of guilt over that feeling.

There were people gathering their things who'd obviously been out here almost all day. Some of them sported tans, while others looked so red they had to be painful. It was clearing out.

It was...nice. Nice to sit here after coming out on a whim. Nice to see the way she sat cross-legged on the beach as if it were the most natural thing in the world to do.

And maybe for her it was. But for him?

Not so natural. But he could see how it could become so. And he'd better enjoy it, because he couldn't see himself coming out here on his own very often. And asking Shanna to join him periodically was... impossible.

He would not...*could* not do that. Because sitting here with her felt natural and good.

Without a word, she unclipped her hair and lay back on the sand and when she did...

Oh, hell. When she did, his body shifted into another gear. One that moved in slow motion and yet seemed to coil in readiness. He tried to stare out over the water as the sun edged lower in the sky, but try as he might, he couldn't stop his peripheral vision from moving back to her and imprinting what it saw on his brain. So he closed his eyes and refused to look. At her. At the sun.

"Zeke, you're going to miss it."

When he peeked, he saw that she was propped up on her elbows rather than stretched out. He wasn't sure that was any better, but if he went back to hiding behind closed lids, she was going to want to know why, and there was no way he was going to tell her the real reason.

"Just enjoying the breeze."

Like hell he was. But she was right. The sun was now a fiery ball in the sky, and it had started painting colors along the horizon, the red tones piling on top of each other until it became a kaleidoscope.

It was so different from the sunrise. Maybe not the colors, but the emotional sensation of a day nearing completion.

He liked it. Maybe too much. "It's beautiful."

"I haven't been out here in forever. I'm glad we came."

"Me, too."

They spent several minutes just watching the sky transform before it started shutting down the show, a heaviness beginning to darken the beach and the water.

Her soft voice came from next to him. "Sometimes you can see dolphins playing near shore. There's nothing like it on earth."

Oh, he could think of a couple of things.

But they weren't things he could admit to himself, much less to her. "I'm sure it's beautiful."

She turned her head to look at him. "It is. It's amazing."

Something about the shadows that played around her cheeks, her eyes—her lips—gave her an air of mystery that made him swallow. "Yes, it is. It's amazing."

They stared at each other for a very long time before he did something he shouldn't. Something that was going to get him in so much trouble.

But it was as if the sunset was reeling him in, whispering that everything would be okay, even when he was pretty sure it wouldn't be. When he reached out and traced his finger over one of her cheeks, she didn't move, eyes still on his.

As if his decision were made, his hand moved to her nape, his palm curving over the soft surface he found there. And then lowering his head, his mouth found hers.

CHAPTER SEVEN

THE TOUCH OF his lips sent her soul soaring into the heavens. She had consciously asked for this, but she knew that something inside her had been hoping this moment would come ever since they'd gotten into his car. She couldn't stop her body from turning toward him, or her arm from reaching up and curling around the back of his neck.

He was as warm as the sand. No. Warmer. And the heat from his body was melding with her own until she couldn't tell where he ended and she began. But what she did know was that there was nowhere she'd rather be than right here. Right now.

And if they stayed like this much longer, she wasn't going to be able to move. Wasn't going to be able to stop...

She didn't want to stop.

But if she didn't…

She might come to care too much. And if he left…

Forcing herself to stop clinging to him, she put an inch between them, then two.

He stared at her for a second before letting her go so fast that she would have fallen back onto the sand if he hadn't steadied her.

"Hell, Shanna, I'm sorry. I have no idea where that came from."

She did. It was the magic of the sun and the water. That's all it was. That *had* to be all it was. Because she didn't want to risk it being any more than that. Her life was good as it was. She was happy with it.

Right?

Yes. She was.

She forced herself to respond to his apology. "It's okay. I'm just as guilty. Let's chalk it up to the sunset. It tends to cast a spell on you."

"Right. The sunset."

But as he dragged his hand through his hair again like he'd done earlier, she sensed he was struggling with something.

Well, so was she and it had nothing to do

with the setting. But she'd better get herself back under control, or she could be setting herself up for a world of heartache. She didn't do relationships. Didn't want to. Some people might get their happy endings, but she and her mom sure hadn't. And the thought of having to go through a pain that great again was too much.

Not that Zeke had even mentioned anything about getting involved or making this into anything other than a silly mistake.

Only it didn't feel silly. So she needed to get up and move before she let herself get swept away again. "Well, it's getting dark. Are you ready to head back to the car?"

"Whenever you are." He stood to his feet and reached a hand down to her.

She hesitated before placing her hand in his and letting him help her up. But thankfully he didn't hold on to her once she was on her feet. In fact he released his grip the second she was up. But where there should have been relief, there was just a sense of emptiness that seemed to drain the beauty from the sunset she'd just witnessed.

Was she doing the right thing by closing

herself off from relationships? The other times she'd gone out on dates she could have definitively said yes. But this time?

And tonight hadn't even been a date.

It was more than that.

The words whispered through her like the warm ocean breeze. A breeze she needed to get out of if she had any hope of walking away from this without embarrassing herself.

They walked to the car in silence and when they got inside, Zeke made no mention of putting the top down, and she was glad. All she wanted to do was get home and forget that kiss had ever happened. Whether that was possible or not was yet to be seen.

All she knew, though, was that she needed to try. Or she might be setting herself up for a world of pain.

Shanna straightened the crown on her head, yet again. Was he going to show?

Fiddling with the display of pumpkins, she wondered if Zeke was going to back out altogether. She hadn't spoken more than ten words to him since he'd dropped her off at her mom's house with yet another apology. Somehow that second "I'm sorry" had been worse than the first. It had a ring of finality to it that had made her face heat.

Every day since then, she'd been tempted to text him and ask if he needed help carving his heart, but didn't trust herself to be around him any more than necessary. And since he hadn't contacted her outside of work, she was afraid any move on her end would have an air of desperation to it.

She'd seen him over the last week, but anytime they'd run into each other, he'd been noticeably standoffish, which made her doubly glad that she'd given him a cheerful wave before walking from his car back to her mom's condo. At least he wouldn't think she'd been hoping for more than a kiss.

Actually, it would be unbearable for him to think that. As it was, her mom had wanted a rundown on all that had happened after they left her place. Shanna had made her explanation as short and succinct as possible, leaving out any and all details that might make her mom think it had been anything other than two colleagues spending a casual hour or two together.

And it was pretty obvious that Zeke regretted what had happened on the beach. Two apologies and a week of avoidance had gotten his message across in no uncertain terms.

He didn't want a relationship, he didn't want friendship. He probably didn't even want to have to work with her anymore. She should be glad.

And she was. Glad the decision had been taken out of her hands.

Her mom said they were still in contact about the condo and were getting the mortgage stuff in order. Things were going swimmingly, according to her mother. Her mouth twisted. She was really glad they'd left her out of it. She hoped the best for him. But right now, the less she had to interact with him, the better. If she were honest with herself, it was a little odd to be on this side of the equation. It was normally her putting the brakes on things with men. And she would have in this instance as well, if Zeke hadn't had his own foot so firmly on them that she could practically smell the rubber burning as the wheels screeched to a halt.

It made her feel foolish and downright stupid.

So, yeah, she wouldn't be surprised if he was a no-show tonight. She tried to figure out how to space the pumpkins a little farther apart rather than leave a blank spot where his would have been.

"I think you're going to have a great turnout tonight as always, Shanna. Congratulations. This may be our biggest night yet." Dan, the hospital administrator stood looking at the lineup of pumpkins.

She smiled at him. "So you're dressed as...let me guess." She put her finger on her lower lip. "A hospital administrator?"

"Very funny. I'm still on duty. I do want people to take me seriously when I'm greeting the patrons and patients alike."

"I know. I'm kidding."

"You, on the other hand...look amazing."

He gripped her hand and held it up as he surveyed her Glinda the Good Witch costume. With its layers and layers of frothy pink tulle and huge puffed sleeves, it was a little harder to walk in than she'd expected it to be. As was the tall pink crown that felt like it might topple off her head at the slightest movement, even though she'd bobby-pinned the heck out of it. Her hand crept up yet again to make sure it wasn't hanging sideways.

Nope. Still there. Which was a little more than she could say for her pride, which still stung.

"Thank you." She made what she thought might be a Glinda-csque curtsy just as the doors opened and in walked a pirate. A tall upright figure that… She blinked, stopping midbow as she realized that was no pirate. It was Zeke, looking incredibly stunning, and nothing like Johnny Depp. With his broad shoulders, he filled out the loose white shirt that he'd cinched with a wide black leather belt, his black jeans not quite what she would envision as pirate gear, but the boots they were tucked into certainly were. God. He looked yummy.

And he was carrying a pumpkin.

All her lies of being glad he might not

come flew out the window. She was glad. Incredibly, irrationally glad. And that made her pull up short.

Realizing she was still holding Dan's hand, she let go and gave him an apologetic smile. "Sorry. I was worried Zeke was going to ditch the event, but it looks like he's brought his entry after all."

"That's a good thing. Especially since I met a young family waiting in line outside who asked for Dr. Vaughan. They were speaking Spanish, but I understood a little of it."

"That's wonderful. Zeke... Dr. Vaughan will be really happy they made it." She wasn't too embarrassed to be caught calling the cardiologist Zeke, since staff members tended to use each other's first names. Dan, obviously, had to be more formal when talking to the public about hospital staff.

Zeke came over to them, taking in both her and Dan. "I ran into traffic, sorry I'm late."

She smiled. He actually didn't seem as distant as he had for the last several days. "I was just about to give up on you."

"Were you?"

She ignored the question, glancing at the black leather bands on both of his wrists and the gold hoop in his ear. Wait… She looked closer. "Did you actually…?" She touched the earring.

"Pierce my ear? No. It screws on the back. I feel a little like my grandmother."

That made her laugh. "Believe me, you don't look like any grandmother I've ever seen."

"Neither do you."

Dan had walked off to greet more of the staff, leaving her to handle Zeke on her own. "Thank you. I think."

"That's quite the outfit. Are you from that kids movie with the ice and the song that everyone was singing for a while?"

"Frozen?" Her brows went up. "No. Try an earlier generation."

He shook his head, looking blank.

Seriously? He didn't know who she was supposed to be?

"It has a tornado? And Kansas, and ruby slippers…"

"Of course. *Wizard of Oz.*"

"Yes. And you're a pirate, obviously." Realizing he was still holding his pumpkin, she motioned him toward the empty spot. "Here, put that down."

When he set the pumpkin in place, her eyes widened. He'd done the diagram of a heart just like he said he was going to do but this... This was great. "Wow. You carved this on your own?"

"I did. It took me almost the whole day yesterday."

"I am seriously impressed. I may have to hand in my carving tools and let you take over my class."

"No thank you. I'm still not comfortable in this getup, but I did like carving the pumpkin. How did Dan get out of dressing up?"

"He says because he's greeting the public and needs to be recognizable. It's the same story every year."

"Funny how that works for him but not for anyone else."

She smiled. "Well, you can't blame him. He has to be ready to answer questions and schmooze with potential patrons. It's kind of hard to do that while dressed as Peter Pan."

Zeke's eyes cut back over to the administrator. "That's an image I won't be able to easily erase."

Neither was the one of Zeke leaning over her on the beach as he got ready to kiss her. He'd been soft and approachable and far too sexy.

But it hadn't lasted. Then again, it was probably better this way. In fact, she knew it was.

"Well, you'd better hang on to that mental image, because that's about as close to a costume as Dan is ever likely to get." She glanced at her watch. "We have about five more minutes before people start filing in."

"What am I supposed to do?"

"Just kind of mill around and be in character, if you can."

"In character. I don't think that's going to work for me. But I can walk around and talk to people. But saying 'Argh, matey!' is out of the question."

"It's okay. Just be you. I don't think I could imitate Glinda's voice very well, either. But I can nod and curtsy enough to get the point across, I hope."

"I'm sure other people are brighter than I am and will get it right off." He glanced at the line of pumpkins. "So I don't need to stay with mine?"

"Nope. They just have numbers on them since we don't really want anyone to know who carved what. Otherwise it could become a popularity contest."

"One I wouldn't possibly have a chance at winning." He grinned.

He was very wrong. Which was why they'd changed the way the contest was run after that first year. Because Zeke could certainly win a popularity contest based solely on who he was. "Don't sell yourself short, Zeke. Cardiothoracic surgeons are always the life of the party, right?"

He leaned closer. "Argh...matey."

That made her laugh, just as the doors opened and people started filtering in, heading straight for the candy line or the pumpkin-carving contest. "That's our cue."

"Okay, see you on the other side."

"Oh, I almost forgot. Marcos will be coming in. Dan saw the family in line outside. He'll be looking for you."

"Okay, thanks. I'll keep an eye out for him." He gave a quick salute and headed off.

Something passed through her head at the speed of light, before she lost whatever it was. About Zeke?

She wasn't sure. But she was glad things weren't as chilly between them as they had been for the last week. Maybe things were looking up. But whatever it was, right now, she just needed to concentrate on her duties and stay in character for the next couple of hours.

Zeke was almost talked out and his bandanna kept sliding down his head, forcing him to push it back up again. He felt ridiculous. Although Shanna had seemed happy enough to see him.

That surprised him after how he'd acted for the last week. It was as if he'd been afraid she would suddenly morph into Kristen and start urging him to give up being a reservist. Actually, he wasn't sure if she even knew he was in the military. He hadn't told her. But he knew how hospital gossip chains were.

That kiss had been an impulsive move. And for someone who rarely did something without thinking it through, it had turned him sideways. But here Shanna was acting as if it had never happened. Maybe he'd made a bigger deal out of it than he'd needed to.

And wow, she looked like she was dressed for a formal ball with that puffy dress on. But it fit her perfectly, as if it had been custom-made with her in mind. He'd had a hard time trying to figure out anything to wear. He'd finally settled on a shirt he'd found at a thrift store and some cheap boots and a bandanna. But there was no way he was wearing striped pants that looked like they belonged in a B pirate movie. He'd also forgone the eye patch. But no one seemed to be looking at him like he was something to be pitied. As far as costumes went, there was a mix of traditional and silly, and he really enjoyed seeing the kids dressed up as different characters.

Then a family came in that he recognized. Marcos and his parents. While his parents were dressed as anything other than themselves, Marcos was wrapped round and round in strips of white cloth. He waved at the boy and his parents, wishing Shanna was there to translate. Instead, he fingered one of the cloth wrappings and gave the boy a smile and a thumbs-up sign. While still thin, the child had a rosier hue to his skin today, hopefully evidence that whatever treatment the pulmonologist had him on was working. At least for now.

It was hard to tell what the future held for the child, but hopefully the parents would get some counseling on how to handle each stage of the disease as it came. The important thing was to be scrupulously consistent with his medications and breathing treatments. It would help hold the disease at bay for as long as possible. If he ended up in the right place at the right time, there was always the possibility of a double lung transplant when his own lungs became too compromised to deliver enough oxygen to his body.

Suddenly Shanna was there, greeting the

parents and smiling at Marcos and gripping his little hand in her own.

"Se ve saludable."

Marcos's mom and dad responded to whatever she'd said with nods.

"Se siente mucho mejor."

She glanced at Zeke. "They said he feels much better."

"I'm happy to hear that."

Shanna translated the words for the family, who nodded with smiles.

She talked to them for a few minutes more, before sending them on their way. "I explained to them how to vote for their favorite pumpkin. They wanted to know which one you made, and I had to tell them it was a secret. Although if they think for a few minutes, they'll figure it out."

"Thanks for rescuing me. I'm taking this as a sign that I might need to learn a second language."

"If you're going to stay here for any length of time, it probably wouldn't hurt. There are a lot of places that teach Spanish."

"I'll keep that in mind." He looked over. "Well, I'll be damned."

Coming down the walkway with a walker, his wife supporting one of his arms, was Mr. Landrum, who'd just been discharged on Friday. To say she hadn't expected to see him was an understatement. Zeke shared her surprise. "Should he be out yet?"

"Probably not, but from what I've learned about him from his family, he's a pretty stubborn guy. Which may be why he survived that surgery, even after all hell broke loose."

"I'm glad he did. Is his insurance going to cover any cardiac rehab?"

"Unfortunately, no. But I'm working on a plan to help with that."

"A plan? What kind of plan?"

Before he was able to say anything else, though, Mr. Landrum reached them, holding his hand out for Zeke to shake.

Zeke looked at him. "Do you think being here tonight is wise?"

"Maybe not. But climbing on that tractor this afternoon was probably not the brightest idea, either."

He felt his face twist in outrage.

Mr. Landrum broke in before he could

respond. "I'm joking. Even I'm not stupid enough to try to go back mowing grass. At least not right now. In a few weeks, it'll be another matter."

"Six weeks. You need six weeks for those bypasses to heal. Six weeks to regain your strength. To do anything before that time is just inviting disaster."

"I hear you. Six weeks. Got it." He glanced to the side. "Now excuse me while I go and vote on pumpkins. I think I may have guessed which one my friendly neighborhood cardiac surgeon may have carved."

"Oh, you do, do you? Well, good luck. I might surprise you."

"You already surprised me. When you did my surgery and gave me my life back. I don't know what I can ever do to thank you."

"You can start by giving yourself time to heal. By not taking on too much too soon."

The man's wife looked at him. "Are you listening, Matthew?"

"I'm sure you're going to remind me again and again."

"Yes, I am, until the message makes it past that thick skull of yours."

"Message heard and received." He gave her a smile that was filled with a mixture of love and exasperation, the way true love should be. "Now can we get off the nagging train?"

"Yes. But when you get too tired, you need to let me know."

He gave her a tired nod. "I think you'll know before I even say a word."

They slowly made their way over to the first pumpkin on the block, waiting behind a line of other people who were also trying to cast their votes.

Shanna said, "Think he'll listen?"

Glancing over at the couple and the way Mr. Landrum's wife had her hand over his on the walker, he nodded. "I think he will. I don't think he has a choice. And honestly, he's a lucky man to have her."

"I was just thinking that very thing."

Their glances caught for a moment or two before breaking apart. He realized what he'd said was true. Matthew Landrum was a very lucky man to have someone who loved him enough to tell him the truth. Who loved him enough to lay down the law in an effort to keep him safe. It didn't mean he'd always do as she told him to do, but what it did mean was that he wasn't going to want to leave her before it was his time to go.

It was a love like his parents had. But how was that love going to look six months from now? A year from now, when the only one who remembered was his mom?

He didn't want to think about what that kind of loss would look like.

Shanna gave them one more look before backing away. "Well, I need to go over to the pumpkins and try to get a preliminary count once the crowds thin out a bit."

"Okay, I'll see you later. Anything specific you want me to be doing?"

"No, just mingle with the crowds. This is supposed to raise community awareness of the hospital's needs. Every year, we seem to get a large grant from someone who goes through the line, but who wishes to remain anonymous. And I think that's partly due to the way the doctors and other staff show they care by being here. Not everyone can or does come to the party."

One brow went up. "It was a pretty strongly worded flyer."

"Yes, it was, but that doesn't mean that people always care enough to participate. Or some have second jobs or pressing family needs and just don't have the time. But for those of us who do, it's an important event in the life of Everly Memorial."

"I'll try to remember that next year."

"See you later. Make sure you stick around to hear final results of the contest."

"Honestly, I don't care if I win or lose. It's been a good experience. Much better than I thought it would be."

The smile Shanna sent him warmed him through and through. And then he walked away and made his way into the crowd, to do one of the things that he liked the least: make small talk with people he didn't know.

Shanna couldn't help it. Her eyes sought him out time and time again, trying to be careful that he didn't catch her looking at him. But, of course, he had a couple of times, earning her either a raised brow or a slow smile that seemed to burn right through her. And each time, she expected to find herself in a fluffy, melted heap on the floor. The change in his attitude from this past week was enough to make her head spin. But who knew how long it would last. She could fall for the man far too easily. And that thought was enough to scare her into averting her eyes. At least for a few minutes.

Somehow she rallied and went about her job, keeping track of the votes tallied up by the various pumpkins. They'd all done a great job. There was Zeke's heart, and Dr. Murphy's depiction of a newborn baby. There were also funny ones like an appendix attached to a string of intestines or even a dog holding a ball.

Everyone had gotten at least one vote, and since the staff weren't allowed to participate in that part of the event, it showed how hard they'd all worked to make this year's Halloween party something that would be remembered for months afterward.

There were only five more minutes of voting left and the crowds had drifted away from the pumpkins and were busy playing the carnival-style games or bouncing in the inflatable house that they'd erected in the courtyard. And the weather had been perfect. Just like that night on the beach. No rain in sight and balmy temperatures that had morphed into a slightly cooler evening that provided some relief to those who were manning the booths outside.

As soon as the winner of the contest was announced, she'd send everyone out of the room so she could turn off the lights and get some pictures of the jack-o'-lanterns in all of their glory, lit by just the glow of their battery-operated tea lights.

And then they'd line those who were in costumes up and get some shots to send to the local news sources. She'd already spotted one of the television news crews wandering around taking videos and pictures of the events.

There was always a tiny spark of pride and thoughts of how much her dad would have enjoyed this night. How he would have put his heart and soul into it, even if he had no skin in the game. Oh, the memories they could have continued to make together if not for that terrible night. If he hadn't had to play the hero. If, instead, he'd been safely at home with his wife and daughter.

But he wasn't, and none of her selfish thoughts were enough to change that. And while his loss still had the power to bring her to tears, she went on doing what she could to try to make him proud of her, wherever he was.

The timer on her watch went off and she went over to the pumpkin display, catching the last few votes as they were cast before putting up a rope in front of the ballot boxes to show that the time had passed to select a winner. Then she and Dan opened each box and pulled out the remainder of the ballots, adding them to the totals they'd tallied earlier and marking them on the sheet she'd made up for that purpose.

"Okay, looks like we have a winner," Dan said. "Are you ready for me to announce it?"

She smiled. "I am."

The hospital administrator climbed onto a small podium, where a band had been playing earlier, pulling the microphone from one of the stands. "Okay, here's the moment you've been waiting for. To see which one of our talented staff carved what you declared as the best pumpkin."

People gathered around as he talked a little bit about the history of the party and named her as the mastermind behind it, something that always made her feel a little uncomfortable, since it really was a team effort. But she smiled and did her best Glinda curtsy, holding her long magic wand out to the side as she did so.

"So if we call your team's name, please come up and collect your prize."

It always struck her as funny, because the prizes were vouchers to the hospital cafeteria, which wasn't really the most popular hangout at the hospital. But Dan had always said it was better to keep the prizes in-house to support the things that they were trying to do and promote.

"In third place, we have Newborn Baby by Dr. Murphy and the Everly Women's Center."

A bunch of hurrahs went up and a cluster

of five people, headed by the ob-gyn herself, Beverly Murphy. They handed out a gift certificate to each team member. Shanna carried the plate containing the pumpkin over to the group so pictures could be taken.

"Congratulations," Dan said. "And now, in second place, we have an unusual entry. Zeus and his Lightning Bolt, carved by the radiology department." That garnered several laughs as people got the connection between the imaging department and a bolt of lightning. She was actually surprised that entry hadn't won the grand prize. It was well executed, and this team had won several years in a row.

Pictures were taken and their prizes were handed out. And then Dan once again brought the microphone to his mouth. "Our grand-prize winner came as a little surprise to me, since Radiology normally has this one in the bag, but I just want to say that it really does fit who we at Everly are as a hospital. I hope we're seen as a place where you are cared for when you're ill. Where you're supported as you heal. And where you're comforted when you grieve. More than anything, Everly has a heart for this community and for you. Our winning pumpkin is The Heart by the newest member of our team, Dr. Zeke Vaughan. Dr. Vaughan, come up here, please."

Shanna looked around to try to see where he was, but there was no movement in the crowd.

Dan glanced at her, and all she could do was shrug. Surely he hadn't gone home. He knew how important this event was to the hospital. Of course, he probably hadn't expected to win. But still. She couldn't see him leaving without stopping to tell her.

Then a voice came from a nurse who was standing by one of the doorways. "Dr. Vaughan has had an emergency and is with a patient."

Shanna's eyes went wide and she searched the crowd for two faces that should be there. She saw Marcos with his parents, but when she looked for Matthew Landrum, she didn't see either him or his wife. Maybe he'd gotten tired and had gone home. But as her eyes scoured the room, she saw a lone walker standing over by a door.

Oh, no! Was that the one he'd used?

She wanted to rush from the room and find that her fears were unfounded. Instead, she had to stand there and do her best to smile as Dan smoothed over Zeke's absence.

"Like I told you, folks, Everly Memorial has a big heart. Our cardiac surgeon is proving that point tonight, by putting his patients first. But we'll get his prize to him. Thank you all for coming out to support the hospital and its mission. And our party is still going strong, so enjoy yourselves and be safe going home. We love you all."

There was clapping as Dan hopped from the podium and came to where she was. "Any idea what happened?"

Shanna blinked moisture from her eyes. "No, not for sure. But one of Zeke's patients—a double-bypass case who came out tonight—is nowhere to be seen, and I think that walker is the one he was using when he came in." She nodded at the wall where the mobility device was still sitting unclaimed.

Dan nodded. "Let me know if you hear anything. I still have to go around and talk to people, but come and find me."

"I will. I need to get pictures—"

"I'll take care of that, Shanna, just go find Zeke."

She found him. Zeke sat in the empty cardiac waiting room, a surgical cap gripped in his hand. He was in scrubs. The boots he'd worn with his costume and that fake earring were the only evidence of the part he'd played less than an hour earlier.

There was a defeated look to the droop in his shoulders and the way he leaned forward as if in physical pain.

Her heart cramped, and she stood frozen for a minute before forcing herself to move.

She touched his shoulder before sitting down beside him. "Hey. Are you okay?"

A muscle worked in his cheek, and she thought for a minute he wasn't going to answer her. A sheet of ice seemed to encase her with a cold she'd never known before. She'd had patients pass away before, but there was something about the way Zeke was just sitting there that told her the outcome wasn't a good one. He shook his head.

"Mr. Landrum?"

"Yes."

"Oh, Zeke, I'm so, so sorry."

"He threw a clot while I was standing there talking to him and his wife. I tried. I opened him up, tried to find it. Dammit. I couldn't. Couldn't find it."

She wanted to weep. What could she say? Certainly nothing that would make him feel any better. Dan Brian was right about one thing. This heart surgeon truly did have a heart.

She put her arm around his neck and laid her head on his shoulder, trying just to be there for him.

His head went back to lean against the chair cushion. She thought her own heart was going to break. That patient had seemed so happy, so alive less than an hour earlier, bantering back and forth with his wife.

"Hell." His voice was rough. Graveled. A sign he was in danger of losing his composure completely. "Any chance we can get out of here?"

If people didn't think doctors mourned over patients, here was a prime example that that wasn't true. There were some people who just made an impact on you, and their loss…

"Absolutely." She would shoot Dan a quick text and let him know what had happened. He would understand. He'd be the first person to tell Zeke to take some time to himself. And the administrator was the consummate professional. He could cover for her and would probably do a better job than she could do herself.

While he got up to throw his soiled scrubs in a receptacle, she sent off a text, letting Dan know what was going on.

Her phone pinged.

Got it. Tell him to take some time. I've got this.

With shaky fingers she typed back.

Thnx.

When Zeke came back, she looped her arm through his. "I know a back way out."

He didn't say anything but let her lead him through a hallway where janitorial supplies were kept near a back entrance, where workers could come and go. She'd needed to leave through this same exit more than once, for this same reason.

Twilight was just falling as they made their way around the deserted side of the building. They'd have to go back to the parking area where they might run into people, but hopefully not anyone who would know either of them.

She found her car and dug for her keys, unlocking it. Zeke hesitated for a second before getting in.

"Do you want me to take you home?" She climbed in her own seat.

He gave a pained snort. "Home. No. The last place I want to go is back to that hotel."

Shanna understood that feeling completely. "Let's go back to my house. I can make you some coffee or tea. Whatever you want." She started the car.

Before she could pull out of the space, warm fingers touched her chin, turning her to look at him. "Why are you doing this? Especially after the way I've acted this last week."

Her chin wiggled for an instant before

she got it back under control. "Because I've been there. I've lost people I care about."

His palm cupped her other cheek, easing her a bit closer until he pressed a kiss on her lips. It was soft and fleeting, but said everything that needed to be said.

Then she put the car in gear and pulled out of the lot, heading…home.

CHAPTER EIGHT

ZEKE LEANED HIS head against the seat rest, trying to get the images out of his head. The ones of soldiers he'd worked on and lost. The cries of pain and fear as they were brought to him in hopes that something could be done. Sometimes it could. Sometimes it couldn't. He'd been to counseling to come to grips with what he'd seen out in the field.

But here he was at a state-of-the-art hospital and he couldn't save a patient he'd worked on eight days ago? A patient he'd almost lost on the table during bypass surgery, but who'd somehow come back from the brink. And look where that had gotten him: lost to a damn clot. Something so ridiculously stupid. It was a gamble anytime surgery was performed, but with each roll of that wheel he hoped for a winning number.

And, damn, he'd wanted Matthew Landrum to win. Had willed his heart to start beating again as he cracked open his chest and performed cardiac massage.

All for nothing.

Shanna hadn't said anything since that kiss a few minutes ago, and he could kiss her all over again just as a thank-you. The last thing he needed was platitudes or words that were meant to comfort him, but which would do the opposite. He needed time to rage in his head against the kind of deity who would give back life only to take it again days later.

What seemed like an hour later, but was probably a lot less than that, she pulled into the driveway of a modest home, pressing a button to open a garage door before driving the vehicle inside.

Without a word, she exited, and he followed suit. What he really wanted to do was lie down and sleep for a while. There was a bone-weariness in him that he hadn't felt in a long time.

She led him through a kitchen to the living room, where she nodded at him to sit, then disappeared into the kitchen. He toed off his boots and propped his feet on the long leather ottoman that sat in front of the couch.

Matthew Landrum's wife was going home to an empty house. Tomorrow she'd be planning a funeral for a man whom she thought would be beside her for years to come. Only he wouldn't be.

How long before he went through that same loss with his dad? He closed his eyes.

Shanna came back in with two cups of coffee. He took one and drank a gulp, the brew burning his throat on the way down and hitting his stomach with a force that he welcomed.

She curled up on the couch next to him, her bare feet peeking out from beneath that ridiculously huge dress. Part of the skirt spilled over onto his thighs, and he stared at it. He pinched a piece of the fabric and rubbed it between his fingers. It was a mixture of scratchy weightlessness that defied explanation.

But maybe some things didn't need explanations.

Like that kiss on the beach?

He took another pull of his coffee and glanced over at her. She'd removed that tall crown thing that had been perched on her head, and her hair was falling out of the clips that she'd used to hold it in place.

And God. She was gorgeous. There was something magical about her that was as inexplicable as her dress. As that kiss on the beach. Something that drew him to her time and time again.

His fingers traced her cheek as she watched him, her own coffee cup in her hand. "Thank you." He nodded at the mug he was holding.

"You're welcome."

But still he didn't pull his hand away, exploring the planes and curves of her jawline to where it met her earlobe, which was heavy with a dangly gold earring. He gently tugged at it, hearing a slight intake of breath as the side of his hand brushed against her throat.

Did she feel it, too? This strange pull of

emotions that seemed to be winding silken threads around him?

"Zeke…" The breathy whisper came just as his fingertip touched her bottom lip. He set his cup on a tray that was lying across the ottoman and slid his fingers into the hair at her nape and tugged her closer.

This time, she was the first to make contact, her mouth sliding onto his with a gentleness that sent his other hand up to cup her face and hold her in place. It was the softest, sweetest touch he'd ever experienced, and his eyes closed to take it in.

Shanna pulled away for a second, like she had at the beach, but when he frowned and opened his eyes, he saw she was just setting her coffee cup on the side table next to the couch.

Then she was back. And this time the kiss was stronger. Warmer. Infused with a sense of urgency that matched the one growing inside him.

And this time, there were no people around. No reason to stop.

He hauled her onto his lap, her poofy skirt enveloping them both. It was heaven and hell all rolled into one sweet package. One he didn't seem to be able to resist.

When their lips met again, her mouth opened with a heady question mark that he was more than happy to answer. His tongue slid against hers, and she made a sound deep in her throat as she shifted on his thighs so that she straddled him.

Oh, hell. The pressure of her against him was almost his undoing. But somehow he held it together as he gripped her hips. The top of her dress clung to her ribs and waist, and he had no idea if he could get it off her.

Or if he even should.

His palms slid up to find her breasts, kneading them. And the answer to her dress was suddenly answered. Yes. He should.

He drew away from her lips, his mouth trailing to her ear. "Is there an easy way to get this dress off of you?"

"No. But nothing good, is ever easy, right?" She gave a soft laugh and nipped at his lips. "There's a zipper in back. Pull it down."

Reaching behind her, he found the little tab and tugged. It slid along the tines much more easily than he'd expected and he got it as far as her waist. Which was all he needed for right now.

He peeled the fabric down her shoulders, past breasts that had no need of a bra.

The sight was his undoing. Pressing his hands against the bare skin of her back, he drew her to his lips and found his first nipple...then closed his eyes as the sensation of tight, puckered skin met his tongue. Oh, yes. She was definitely all heaven. At least right at this moment.

Drawing her deeper in his mouth, he reveled in the way her back arched and she moaned, her hands holding him to her as if afraid he might leave.

Hell, he wasn't planning on going anywhere.

Except here. His hands tunneled beneath all of that fluffy fabric until he somehow managed to find the bare skin of her thighs, gliding up them until he reached the edge of panties that were warm and silky. Some kind of lace.

His thumb eased under the elastic at one leg and encountered a moist heat that made his body tighten with need. A need so sharp that he ached to finish it now. But he couldn't, not yet. He touched the juncture of her thighs, and she shuddered against him, as if she felt the exact same thing.

As he moved to yank his wallet from the back of his jeans, he let go of her breast so he could find what he was looking for. At least he hoped it was there.

There. He pulled the packet free, even as Shanna stood to her feet.

He looked up at her, wondering if she was calling a halt to things, but instead, she reached under her skirts and pulled her panties down, kicking them to one side, her breasts jiggling in a way that made his mouth water.

Then instead of taking her dress off the rest of the way, she lifted her skirt around her hips. "Put it on." She smiled and looked at the packet.

Ripping it open, he eased his zipper down and released himself, then slowly rolled the condom down his length.

Shanna's teeth came down on her lower

lip. Then with skirts still gathered in her fists, she climbed back on top of him.

"You're going to keep that on?"

"You object to role-playing?"

Hell, when she said it like that, no he did not.

The skirts fell around their hips, and she reached under them and found him, taking him in hand and stroking in a way that made everything in him rise up in a rush.

His hands went to her breasts, still bared to him, and he murmured, "I need to be inside of you, Shanna. Soon."

"How about right now?" The hand that was stroking kept going, but her body shifted, edging up and forward until he felt that same heat he'd touched earlier. Slowly she eased onto him, sliding down in a single smooth motion, and he jerked with pleasure when she reached the bottom. Her hands came out from beneath her skirts and untied the ties at the neck of his white shirt, her fingers curling around his bare shoulders.

"Hell, Shanna."

She rose and fell, her eyes on his face as she squeezed around him. But it wasn't enough. He needed more. His hands went to her waist and moved her with purpose. Deeper, harder, his own hips lurching up with each downward movement. He pressed her breasts to his face as he breathed in her scent.

Then he could stand it no more. He carried her down to the couch, so that she was on her back, and he was in between her thighs, the costume making things even hotter, although he had no idea how that was possible.

Her feet pressed against the arm of the sofa as he thrust into her over and over, mouth meeting hers and kissing her with a ferocious need that he couldn't remember ever feeling before. One arm went under her hips, tilting them up to change the angle. She immediately went still and moaned, then began pumping her hips wildly against him. He couldn't tell where she started and he ended, until she gave a long, keening cry and strained against him. Then he felt it. That crazy pulsing of her body that traveled up his shaft and pushed him over the edge in a single thrust. He drove into her again and again until there was nothing left.

Then slowly, with a stealth that caught him unawares, the urgent need morphed into a slow, sated calm that took over his body. Took over his mind.

Hell. What had just happened?

He had no idea, but suddenly he was exhausted. Somehow he managed to shift their positions until she was lying on top of him, his arm wrapped around her and holding her against him.

All he could feel was his breath, moving in and out of his body, releasing the tension of a day that had gone so horribly wrong. He let his eyes close. Not to sleep. He just wanted to lie here for a minute and absorb all that she was and all that had happened on this couch.

Just another minute or two and then he'd get up.

Shanna was up and showered by the time he woke up. She'd lain there for almost a half hour watching him sleep, before realizing she was dangerously close to falling for this man.

But why not? She'd seen the best and worst of him.

At least she thought she had.

And she trusted him. Her dad's death and her mom's resultant depression had given her more than enough reasons not to venture into serious relationships, but this was different. Zeke wasn't likely to encounter a land mine in Tampa or be ordered to work under dangerous conditions.

But she needed to give herself a little more time to be sure. Right now her emotions were all jumbled up over what had happened last night. Both to Mr. Landrum and what had occurred in her house.

She knew that when faced with trauma, sometimes the body craved a proof of life that could only be achieved one way. Zeke couldn't be blamed for doing what his instincts told him. And she'd been just as eager.

Neither one of them had stopped to think about what happened afterward. Or how they would handle it. It would be so much easier if they'd gone to his place, so she could slip away before he woke up. But that would be cowardly.

Especially if she was wanting to test the waters and see how dangerous they felt.

They were both adults. They could face what had happened. Right?

At least she was now fully dressed in normal clothes, since she needed to be at work in an hour. She was going to have to wake him up soon, though, because she was his ride.

Ugh!

Tiptoeing back to the living room, she startled when she realized his eyes were open and he was looking straight at her.

She licked her lips. "Hi."

"Hi, yourself." At least he had the throw she'd tossed over him in the middle of the night, because as she'd found out last night, a naked Zeke was damned near irresistible.

She waited for him to say something further, but when he remained silent, she couldn't stop the question. "Are you okay? After everything that happened at the hospital, I mean."

His eyes closed for a second or two before they opened again. "Not quite. But I can't change anything. At least not about that. What I am sorry for is what happened here. I honestly did not come here with any intentions other than to find someplace to decompress. I'm not sure how that all changed."

It was what he needed.

And if she was honest with herself, it was what she'd needed as well, after fantasizing about him at that condo. Not to mention that tantalizing kiss on the beach afterward, which had given her even more material for her dreams.

But the reality of what had transpired last night had blown her dreams out of the water. Sex with him had been so much better than anything she could have imagined.

"I was just as guilty as you, so no apology needed. But I do have to be at work in an hour. I can fix you some breakfast, if you'd like."

"No need. I'll just grab something at the hotel."

"About that... Do you want me to drop

you off there at the hotel? Or at the hospital to get your car?"

He blew out a breath. "Another thing I'd forgotten. I didn't drive here." He seemed to think for a minute. "I don't have anything pressing this morning. If you could just take me to the hospital, I'll go home and change and then come back."

"Okay."

She frowned. They were tiptoeing around each other in a way that felt awkward after her thoughts about romance and whether or not it was possible with him. He was kind of making her feel like it wasn't. Or at least that it wasn't what he wanted. After all, did you really apologize if you were hoping things would continue in the same vein?

She knew nothing about his life before he'd come to the hospital other than the fact that he'd lived in the Panhandle before moving to Tampa. Had he ever been married?

Divorced?

Well, she was pretty certain that he wasn't currently married, but his relationship status really was something she should have asked before she hopped into bed with him.

But people had short flings all the time, right? This wasn't any different from that. In fact, it was easier, because then there was nothing waiting to surprise her around the bend. Not that there would be. The other guys she'd been involved with had been marvelously simple. But the attraction had fizzled out almost before it began.

"Do you want to shower?" she asked.

"Yes, if there's time."

"There is." At the moment, she was more worried about dropping him off by his car, where people coming into work could see them and jump to all kinds of conclusions. And more and more she was thinking they would be the wrong conclusions.

Before she could move away, though, he reached up and wrapped an arm around her, hauling her down to sit beside him. She looked at him in surprise, unable to think past the fact that he was naked under that blanket.

"I know this was all kind of crazy, but when we both have a spare moment, I'd like to sit down and talk about what happened."

"Talk?"

"Yes. About where we go from here. What it all means."

Okay, so it didn't sound like he just wanted to skedaddle out of here and never mention this again.

And where they went from here? Did that mean what it sounded like?

Her thoughts swirled around and around going nowhere, so she finally just said, "I think that's a good idea. Let me know when you have some free time."

"Can we go to dinner somewhere tonight?" He gave her a slow smile. "Especially since our last dinner plans never happened."

They hadn't. Because they'd wound up at the beach instead.

So yes. Dinner sounded promising. Much more so than "I have a space from four to four fifteen free—why don't we talk then."

"I would like that."

With that, he dropped a kiss on her temple and then stood up, the blanket falling away to reveal skin as bare as it had been last night. She gulped as he gathered his clothes from the floor. That was her signal to get the hell away from him before she ended up being late for work and had a whole lot more explaining to do.

Why the hell was he so nervous?

Maybe because this was the first time since Kristen had walked out on him that he was actually entertaining the thought of getting involved with someone again.

And was he entertaining that idea?

He thought so. But this time they'd opted to meet at the restaurant, and Zeke was not going to count on sex after their meal. In fact, it would probably be better if they didn't wind up in bed.

He didn't see any sign of her car in front of La Terrazza, the place they'd planned on eating at a week ago.

Just then his phone pinged.

Am inside. Fourth booth on the right.

Okay, she must have parked behind the restaurant.

I'm here. See you inside.

As soon as he entered the restaurant, his eyes found her. And she looked just as good as she ever did. She'd changed from her scrubs into a pair of dark jeans and a navy gauzy tunic that she'd cinched at her waist with a metal link belt. Her hair was swept back into a high, sleek ponytail that looked both classy and casual. She gave him a quick wave as if unsure whether he'd spotted her.

He had. And he found himself smiling as he strode toward her table.

"I'm not late, am I?"

"No, I'm just a little early."

He slid into the booth and nodded at her glass. "What are you drinking?"

"I'm kind of a stickler about not drinking and driving so it's sweet tea. But you can have whatever you want."

"Tea sounds good."

As if summoned, a waitress appeared to take his drink order and handed him a menu. "Another sweet tea, coming up. Do you need a few minutes?"

"Please."

She left and Zeke opened the menu only

to find that the names of the dishes were in Spanish, even though the descriptions were in English.

He glanced at her. "Any suggestions?"

"The red beans and rice are kind of a Cuban staple. So is the *ropa vieja*."

He had no idea what she'd just said, but the way it rolled off her tongue was sexy as hell. "The rope what?"

She laughed. Also sexy. And a torpedo to his senses in more ways than one, when he'd hoped to keep his wits about him. *"Ropa vieja."* She said the words slowly this time. "It actually translates as 'old clothes' in English, but believe me, it tastes nothing like that. It's unapologetically Cuban. And delicious."

"Okay, then that's what I'll have."

Their waitress returned to the table, and Zeke sat back as Shanna ordered their food in Spanish, carrying on a short conversation with the waitress, who chuckled at something she said. When she left to turn in their order, Zeke was tempted to ask if they'd been laughing at him, before deciding he was being a little paranoid. So instead, he said, "I like hearing you speak Spanish. Did your dad understand the language?"

She gave a half shrug that made her ponytail swish. "He understood more than he spoke, but my memories of him are from my childhood, so it could be skewed a bit. But I'm sure he knew at least some words, since my mom spoke Spanish quite a bit at home."

"You're lucky. I always thought it would be nice to be bilingual."

"It's definitely an advantage in Florida." She smiled again and canted her head to the side. "You don't speak anything besides English?"

"Unfortunately, no. I know words here and there in a few other languages but don't have any extensive knowledge of them."

"I get it. It was hard for my mom to start speaking exclusively in English after she met my father."

"But they made it work."

"Yes, they did."

He hesitated, but didn't want to go through a stilted meal while an elephant lounged on the sidelines waiting to be noticed. "How did they, coming from two different worlds?"

She sighed and seemed to think for a few minutes. "They did come from different worlds and had some barriers to overcome, but they loved each other enough to make those things kind of slide away. Stay out of reach, unless they had a disagreement. Then they never let those times get in the way of the good. Their good times. My parents loved each other despite everything that might have stood in their way. Until he died."

"And your mom didn't regret being with a man who ultimately couldn't stay with her?"

She took a breath before blowing it out. "My mom really struggled after my dad died. So much so that it's made me wary of relationships. Are your parents still together?"

He twisted his lips trying to decide how much to answer, before realizing he needed to tell the truth. It might make a difference in how she saw him. Especially since he was thinking about going out with her periodically. He hadn't been diagnosed yet when Kristen left and he was pretty sure that would have been another strike against him.

He chose his words carefully. "They are still together. But my dad was diagnosed with Alzheimer's a couple of years ago. It's progressed enough that he's not always sure of who people are and it's starting to get noticeable in his speech. He has trouble choosing his words sometimes."

"Oh, Zeke, I'm so sorry. Where do they live?"

"In Jacksonville at the moment, but I'm hoping to convince them to move to Tampa in the near future. In fact, I was thinking about that other condo that was for sale on the ground floor."

"Right, that would be perfect, if he has mobility issues."

He put his straw in his drink and took a quick sip. "Yes, that's exactly what I thought."

"It must be hard for your mom."

"It is. Just like your dad dying must have been hard for you and your mom."

"It was pretty devastating. My mom went through a period of depression after he passed away."

He nodded. "My dad hasn't passed yet, but there are times when it seems like the person he was when I was a kid is no longer there. And that's the hard part, I think, for her. She loves him deeply, but I'm not sure that's something he necessarily understands, nor can he reciprocate."

He hoped that made sense.

"I can see how it would be really hard."

The waitress came back with their food in record time, setting the dishes in front of them with a warning that they were hot.

He waited until she was gone before smiling. "But that's not why I wanted to come to dinner with you."

"No? I was so sure that you wanted to pry all of my family's secrets out of me."

He leaned forward. "I'm not concerned with your family's secrets. I'm only interested in you."

And there. He'd said it. Hopefully there wasn't a stalkerish feel to his words.

"Are you?" Her finger reached out to trail

down the hand he'd placed on the table. It was enough to send a shudder through him.

"Yes." He hurried to add, "But I'm not trying to rush you into anything. I'm just hoping you might want to go out periodically and see where things lead. No pressure. No hurry. I've been in a bad relationship once before and so I'm a little more cautious on that front."

"I hear you. And I'm in favor of everything you just said about going out but keeping it casual. At least for now."

Hmm... He didn't remember anything about it being necessarily casual. But she was probably being the smart one in wanting to go even slower than he might have been thinking. "So...parameters?"

She laughed. "Now you sound like a heart surgeon."

"Do I?" Something about the way she said that amused him. "Does that surprise you?"

"Not at all. In fact, it kind of turns me on."

Okay, now he was in danger of not getting through this meal at all. And as much he'd love to just say to hell with it and drag her back to his hotel for another dose of what they'd had the last time they were together, he really did want to be smart about this.

As if she sensed something in his manner, she added, "But I really do want you to try the *ropa vieja*. After all, if you don't like Cuban food, we may as well just call it quits."

And just like that, she'd steered them back into safer waters. Where they could hopefully get to know each other a little better, and he could find out whether these feelings that had begun to percolate inside him were worth pursuing, or whether they should stop while they were ahead—before they ruined their chance to at least maintain a professional relationship.

His first bite of meat surprised him. It was bold and full of spice and flavor that reminded him of Shanna. It was deliciously different. And he liked it. A lot.

Liked her. A lot.

"So?" She was looking at him with an expectancy that made his chest tighten.

"I love it."

She seemed to relax into her seat. "I am so glad. Not everyone likes rice and beans."

"Well, I haven't tried those yet. But I do like both of those things, and if they're even half as good as the meat is, then I'm going to be a fan for life."

By the time he finished the meal, he could definitely say he was a fan. Of both the meat and of Shanna. She was sweet and funny and seemed so very real. But there was an underlying sensuality that made him sit up and take notice time and time again. And if he hadn't declared sex off-limits for at least tonight, they would have wound up back in each other's arms. But instead, he settled for getting to know her better. And hopefully in the process was laying a more solid foundation than the one he'd had with Kristen.

A foundation that wouldn't be washed away with the first wave that might come their way.

CHAPTER NINE

SHANNA WAS STILL feeling weirdly satisfied as she headed into the hospital eager to see her first patient of the day. Their dinner last night had been a huge success. And for the first time in her life, she felt like she might have found something real with a man. Something she might actually want to hang on to for a while.

Or maybe even…forever.

Was it even possible? Was this how her mom had fallen in love with her dad? Because Shanna couldn't definitely say she was pretty near admitting to herself that she might just care deeply about Zeke.

She turned the corner to head to the elevator, realizing she'd wound up in the hallway that recognized those who had served in the armed forces. But for once it didn't send a chill through her. Maybe because of what was blossoming between her and Zeke. She let herself look at them for once.

There weren't a whole lot of pictures. Maybe fifteen or so out of hundreds of employees. But her gaze stopped on a man who was screwing something into the wall at the far end. A hook. Maybe they had a new hire that used to be in the military.

She started to steer around him when she caught sight of something lying on the ground. A picture of a man in uniform. She was almost past the workman when something stopped her, and she looked again.

There was something about the posture and the slight crease on the left cheek of his serious, unsmiling face. A sense of foreboding rose up within her and she couldn't make her glance go any higher, as she tried to suck down a quick breath or two. Then she realized how weird it must seem for her to just keep standing there. So she forced herself to look at the image again, focusing on the man's eyes. She swallowed and a clawing sense of fear and panic suddenly overwhelmed her.

God! It was Zeke. A little younger than he was now, but still very recognizable.

Despite that dinner last night, she still knew so very little about him. She tried to itemize what she knew. He'd had a bad relationship, which made him wary. *Check.* His dad had Alzheimer's, a terrible diagnosis that had pulled at her as he'd described him to her. *Check.* He'd come from the Panhandle. *Check.* A place where there were military bases. *Check and double check.*

How stupid could she be? It all made sense.

She licked her lips, trying to think. It wasn't like he'd lied to her, or avoided telling her. The subject had just never come up.

But when he'd been discussing loans with her mom, shouldn't he have mentioned that he qualified for VA financing? Maybe he had done that over the phone or something. Or maybe he wasn't even in the military anymore. Could it be that simple?

She cleared her throat. "These pictures are all of men who are no longer active duty, right?"

He shrugged. "I'm just paid to hang the pictures. I don't know anything about them."

"Okay, thanks."

That had to be it. There was no way they could work for the hospital and still be active duty, right? This was just a way of recognizing past service.

But she wouldn't know for sure...unless she asked him.

Over another dinner?

And what was she going to say if he was still somehow connected with the armed forces? But again, she didn't see how he could be anything but discharged. And it had to be an honorable discharge, or they wouldn't hang him up, right?

But it still felt like he'd hidden something important from her. Probably not on purpose. Maybe he just thought she wouldn't care. But then again, she hadn't told him about her dad, either. Just that he had died. Not how he'd died.

Why wait for dinner? Maybe she should just go see him now and discuss it. Tell him what had happened with her dad and give him a chance to open up about his own time in the service. She'd sworn to herself she would never date anyone in the military. At least no one who could actually see combat. She snorted. Her dad had been on a peace-keeping mission. It hadn't even been a war zone. And he'd still died.

Unless the person in the picture was somehow miraculously not Zeke Vaughan, she was going to have a serious problem. Except, she knew in her heart of hearts exactly who it was. There was no nameplate on the picture, but all the rest of them had one, identifying the branch, dates served and their rank.

Before she could stop herself, she knelt down by the framed print and looked at it closer.

The guy stopped working and glanced at her for a second.

She pulled in a deep breath. "Is there a nameplate that goes with this one, too?"

He looked down and pointed at the box on the other side of him. "It's probably still in there. They all have one."

Feeling a sense of doom, she shifted until she could reach the flat box, teasing one of the flaps open. Yes, it was there. But it was upside down. Suddenly she didn't want to turn it over. Didn't want to know. But how did that saying go? With knowledge comes power. Or something like that.

Would it matter if he was no longer serving?

No. Of course it wouldn't. He'd gotten out. He had to have. And unless he was thinking of reenlisting, then it was all fine. They could still go forward with their plan for dating.

So why was she shaking so hard?

Because she'd just met a guy who had swept her away. That had shown a depth of emotion and sensitivity that had eaten away the foundations of the walls surrounding her heart. Had taken away some of the fear of losing someone.

She flipped the nameplate over. It was indeed Zeke. Ezekiel Manning Vaughan, to be exact. She smiled at his middle name. It fit him.

She looked at the rest of the plaque. Field surgeon with a rank she didn't recognize. But when she reached the end of the nameplate, she froze. United States Army Reserves. There was a beginning date, but nothing but a hyphen after that. There was no ending date.

Because he was a *reservist*.

Her eyes closed. She knew what that meant. He could be called back to duty at any time. In fact, it almost certainly meant that he would be deployed from time to time and had to go in for periodic training.

Deployed. For missions?

She dropped the plate back into the box and looked into the face on that picture.

Why hadn't he told her at dinner? It would have made everything so much easier. She could have held up her hand and told him she'd heard enough. That they couldn't date. Casually or otherwise.

Really, Shanna? Would it really have been that easy?

No. Of course not. But the fear was still there, swimming around her insides like it was there to stay. The fear that she could wind up just like her mom, mourning a husband who had died. The fear that she would fall in love with him only to someday have two uniformed men knock on her door and tell her how sorry they were, but that her husband had sacrificed himself... had been a hero. And if they had a daughter, she would be just like Shanna, dragging down the stairs in her ridiculous too-big pajamas and overhearing everything.

A wall of emotion rose up within her.

She couldn't do it.

She stood up and straightened her clothes. She needed to go see him in his office, if he was there. Tell him about her father. And then explain why she couldn't be involved with him, unless he was looking to exit the reserves in the next little while.

Except they wouldn't have hung that plaque if his discharge was imminent, would they?

There was only one way to find out.

Shanna's text was terse, consisting of only three words. Can we talk?

He thought they'd already talked. At dinner last night. Unless she'd had second thoughts.

And that was going to be a problem, because he cared about her. Way more than he should, despite everything he'd said about wanting to take things slow. For the first time, he wanted to keep seeing a woman. What he'd said was true. He wanted to take things slow. But hell, if she suddenly didn't, it was going to be a blow. A big one.

Because whatever this was with Shanna was different. He loved her joie de vivre, her zest and passion for her work and for life in general. He wasn't sure what was happening between them, but knew he wasn't ready for it to end. For the first time since Kristen had walked out on him, he wanted to be in a relationship.

Did he love her?

Maybe, but what if he was wrong about everything?

What if he was making another huge mistake? What if they both were, and she ended up walking away without a backward glance? His insides curdled, turning what he'd eaten that morning rancid.

So what to do about her text? All he could do was answer it.

I'm free now, if you are.

His phone pinged a second later.

On my way.

He started counting, somehow thinking that the seriousness of whatever this was might be able to be measured by how long it took her to get to his office.

He got to twenty before the knock came at his door. It was serious.

Taking a bracing breath, he said, "Come in."

She slid into the room with a stillness that sent a chill through him. There was no sign of the woman who had joked about role-playing and who'd taken him to places he hadn't known existed. No sign of the woman who said if he didn't like Cuban food, they were finished. No sign of the woman who had softly kissed him last night before she got into her car to leave.

Shanna sat.

He waited. And waited.

A minute later, she drew a deep breath. "You mentioned you'd lived in the Panhandle before moving to Tampa. Did you work at a hospital there?"

"At times."

"What does that mean exactly? *Where* did you work?"

Why was she asking about that? Whatever it was, he sensed this was not the time to beat around the bush or give her vague answers. Although he didn't see how any of it mattered unless her belief system somehow didn't allow for military service. He tried again. "I was a combat field surgeon, then when back in the States I worked at a military hospital."

She swallowed visibly. "Why didn't you tell me this last night?"

"It didn't seem relevant to our conversation. Is it?"

She slowly nodded. "Maybe not to you. But it is to me. I told you my dad died when I was a kid."

"Yes."

She bit her lip as if not sure exactly what she wanted to say or how to say it. "I can still picture where I was when I heard the news. I remember my mom crying. I came downstairs and saw men in uniforms standing in our living room. They were awkwardly patting her on the shoulder. And I knew then and there that something horrible had happened. To my dad. They mentioned sacrifice and how he'd saved other people." Her chin trembled. "He wasn't supposed to die. He was on a peacekeeping mission and instead ended up being blown up."

His insides twisted. He had a feeling he knew exactly where this was going. "I'm so sorry, Shanna. I can't imagine being a child and learning about my dad that way."

"I like you, Zeke. A lot. But…"

His brows went up. "But?"

"How long will you be in the reserves?"

Memories of his arguments with Kristen came roaring back. Arguments he never wanted to have again. He kept his voice very soft as he answered. "My contract is for four years."

"Four…" She stopped, her eyes closing for a few seconds before looking at him again. "And you can be called into active duty at any time during those four years?"

He eyed her. "It's a possibility, yes." He

leaned across the desk. "Shanna, I'm sorry about what happened to your dad, and I understand what you must be—"

"I'm not sure you do. Can you guarantee that you won't die on some road on the other side of the world?"

She knew he couldn't. No one could.

"You know I can't promise that. But I was a field surgeon. That's different from being a soldier who goes into battle."

"That's just it. My dad wasn't supposed to be going into battle, either."

"I'm still trying to figure out exactly what this means. Are you saying you don't want to date me now that you know?"

If she was going to ask him to leave the reserves, he couldn't. Not without a valid reason, and he didn't think *my girlfriend doesn't want me to serve* qualified any more now than it had when Kristen had asked him to leave the military.

Wasn't this what he'd dealt with last time? And he and Shanna weren't even serious yet. But he'd wanted to get there.

And now? He was having some serious reservations.

"I don't know what I'm trying to say. I just feel like this came out of nowhere."

He took a deep breath. "Listen, I know it's scary. I know what you went through hurt, and I'm not trying to discount any of it. But my service means a lot to me. It means a lot to my dad, who can barely even recognize me now..." He drew a deep breath. "Even if I wanted to, I can't get out of my contract, Shanna. Can you somehow see past this and still give us a chance?"

Her eyes filled, a single tear coursing down her cheek that turned his insides to an agonizing fire he felt sure would consume him.

"I can't, Zeke. I'm so, so sorry, but I just can't." She stood and swiped at the moisture on her cheek.

He tried to reach out one last time. "Maybe talk to your mom about your dad and ask if she'd do it all over again, if she had the chance."

"None of that really matters now. Because it changes nothing. He died. And she suffered horribly."

She was right. They could talk about

what-ifs all day long, but when it came down to it, if she wasn't willing to take the risk, then they might as well throw in the towel before they even got started.

"I'm sorry, Shanna."

"So am I. This isn't easy."

And yet it seemed like it was. At least for her. Maybe he could at least affirm her in her decision, so they could both move on.

"Since it seems there's nothing left to say, let's forget last night ever happened and go back to the lives we'd planned to live. Agreed?"

"Agreed." As she walked to the door, he murmured, "I'm sorry about your dad, Shanna. I truly am. I have a feeling a lot of his best traits show up in you."

As soon as she left the room, he sank back in his chair and pressed his fingers to his eyelids to keep his own emotions in check. And with that, he picked up the phone and dialed a familiar number.

When she answered, it took him a minute to respond in a voice he hoped passed as normal. "Hi, Mom. How's Dad?"

He listened as she talked for a few minutes, putting a positive spin on most of it. But then again, that was his mom. She'd always been a glass-half-full type of person. When she turned the conversation back toward him, asking how he was, he suddenly knew what he wanted to do. What he *needed* to do.

"Would it be okay if I came home for the weekend?"

"Of course it would be. Is everything okay?"

His teeth clenched for a second. "Things here are okay. I'm just homesick and want to see you both."

"Oh, honey. You know you can always come home. Always."

He needed to end this conversation before she realized everything around him was falling apart. "Okay. I'll see you tomorrow."

Shanna barely made it out of his office before she had to rush to the bathroom and lock herself in a stall as more tears silently dripped down her cheeks. How could something that had looked so promising end so badly? And yet he'd said he could see her dad in her without ever having known him.

If she'd known who he was from the very beginning would she have kissed him on the beach? Slept with him? *Fallen* for him?

Because she knew without a doubt she had. Fallen for him. Head over heels. Only to have everything derailed by one tiny omission. Two, really. Because if she had shared how her dad had died, he might have told her he was still in the service and things would have ended with a smile and handshake.

Except when she had stumbled on him in the waiting room, looking so defeated after Matthew Landrum's death, how could she say that the outcome wouldn't have been the same? That they wouldn't have slept with each other?

But at least then she would have known the score. Would have known it really was just a fling.

You can't help who you fall in love with.

Maybe not, but you sure as hell could decide whether or not you acted on it.

And to have to give his heart patients breathing treatments, knowing that at any moment Zeke could walk in and stir up feelings that were almost unbearable, made her cringe.

He might never be called to duty. Maybe she'd been stupid in talking to him before having all of her facts straight.

She should talk to someone about what being in the reserves actually entailed.

Making two phone calls only made her shoulders dip. Yes, they could be deployed. Sometimes overseas and sometimes they could be sent to national disaster areas within the United States. That she could have handled. But the possibility of losing him in either one of those scenarios?

He'd told her to talk to her mom. But she couldn't. Not right now. Maybe in a few weeks when the dust in her heart had settled a bit.

In the meantime, she wanted to talk to Dan Brian about an idea she'd had a while ago and see if he might be interested.

"So you would work some days at the hospital and some days out in the community, is that what you're saying?"

"Yes. As you know, I'm licensed as a home health respiratory therapist as well as hospital work. Would there be any grant money that could go toward some kind of clinic? Even just in a rented building or a mobile unit that could act as a clinic? Kind of like the blood banks do?"

Dan twirled a pencil, stopping periodically to jot notes to himself. She sure hoped those notes were about what they were discussing. "This couldn't happen right away, you understand. I'll need to research it and see if there are precedents anywhere in Florida."

"So it could take how long, do you think?"

"I'm thinking a year or two." He frowned. "You're not thinking of quitting, are you, Shanna? We'd sure hate to lose you."

And she'd hate to leave the hospital. But right now, the options were stay and wait. Or stay...and stay.

"I'm not thinking about it. But I would sure like to get out into the community. The Halloween event is great, but I also want to do some practical stuff for people who can't afford treatments or medications."

"I get it. And we do have a safety net of sorts. It's just not as good as we'd like it to be, yet."

"I understand. If you can just check into it and let me know if there's hope, or if it's an impossible task. I know you'll give me an honest answer either way."

He nodded, eyes narrowing. "Is there something behind this? Something I can help with?"

Could he somehow change that plaque under Zeke's picture and give it an ending date that wasn't four years away?

Glinda certainly could have. But unfortunately, unlike the good witch, she didn't possess any magical powers. Other than to fall in love with the wrong man.

Only he wasn't the wrong man. He was just in a profession that had caused her and her mom such pain. Well, she'd just have to see how the next week or so went and see if there were ways to avoid working directly with him.

Zeke was gone.

When she got to work Monday morning

and heard he wasn't there, she was sure he'd been called to duty.

Her heart squeezed. And if he was?

Oh, God. What if he was?

"Do you know when he'll be back?"

"I'm not sure," Maura said. "He's asked the hospital to reroute his cases to Dr. Bernard at County General."

"And you don't know where he went?"

Maura looked at her a little closer. "I don't know. I just know it was sudden."

Was it because of what she'd said to him in his office? Could he actually ask to be deployed? Was that even a thing?

The panic from seeing his picture in that hallway rose up in her again. "Okay, thanks. I just wasn't sure what to do with any of his cases."

"As far as I know, he has nothing pending. Maybe check with Pulmonology." Maura smiled. "I'm sure they have plenty to keep you busy."

She was sure they did. But they couldn't keep her mind from running through some pretty horrific scenarios. Like what if he weren't even in the United States anymore?

She had no idea how she'd even go about contacting him.

And why would she need to? Hadn't they said everything that needed saying?

She thought they had. Until now.

He'd told her to go and talk to her mom. Maybe that's exactly what she should do.

"Thanks, Maura. I'll check with them."

As soon as she could get away for the day, she headed for her mom's house. But the second she opened the door, the floodgates opened and, try as she might, she couldn't get them closed again.

Her mom dragged her into the house, folding her in her arms. "What is it?"

"I… It's Zeke." Her voice shook so hard, she could barely get the words out.

"Oh, honey. Is he okay?"

She shrugged, then realizing her mom might think the worst, she managed to get out, "As far as I know he is, but…"

"Tell me what's going on."

"I think I did something stupid. Really stupid."

Her mom eased her over to the couch and

helped her down onto it. "I'm sure whatever it is can be undone."

"I don't think this can."

"Are you pregnant?"

Her eyes widened. "Of course not."

Leave it to her mom to pretty much know where things stood between her and the surgeon.

"Well... You care about him, don't you? And although he hasn't said anything, I'm pretty sure he cares about you."

"I don't see how that will make any difference at this point. I—I just can't be with him."

Her mom rolled her eyes. "That tells me exactly nothing. Unless he's been diagnosed with some horrible disease and only has a few months to live, then..."

He hadn't. But his dad had been diagnosed with one. The thought made her feel even worse.

"Mom, can you sit down for a minute?"

Her mom perched on a chair across from her and watched her. "Okay. I'm ready."

"Zeke is in the army reserves."

She blinked. "So?"

Her mom didn't see what the problem was.

As if hearing her thoughts, she went on. "Shanna, where is this going?"

She took a deep breath. "I have kind of a weird question to ask you. It's about Dad. We never really talked about what happened the day he died."

"I know. You were only ten. And you can't know how many times I tried to look at that day through your eyes, and it's just so terrible. To have found out that way. And then I had to get help…"

The thought of making her mom relive that time almost made her back out of asking the question Zeke had suggested she ask. But she had to know. She reached and grasped her mom's hand. "What advice would you have given Dad back then if you could foresee the future? Foresee what would happen to him?"

Her mom gripped her hand back. "I would have told him to be more careful. But he had an injured buddy in a truck nearby and was anxious to get him back to the base. Only the bomb went off and killed him. But his friend lived. And knowing that would have made him happy."

It wasn't quite what she was looking for. "If you knew ahead of time that Dad would die, would you have married him? Would you have asked him to leave the military?"

Her mom's head tilted. "Oh, honey. No. I would never have asked that. He loved his job more than anything except us. If you're asking if I have regrets over marrying him, no. Not one. Even after what happened. I had your father for twelve wonderful years. That's more than some people ever get."

For some reason that didn't help her. She didn't want Zcke for one year or four... But she also realized how wrong it was for her to even hint that he should try to get out of his contract. That's not what love was. Love meant sacrifice. Loving someone so much that you want the very best for them. Even if it meant their death.

How many firefighters had run into burning buildings only to never reemerge? How many people died every day during the course of doing their jobs or even just helping others?

She'd made this all about her and her fears and had thought very little of the whys behind what Zeke did. Zeke's patient had died, devastating him. But did that mean he wouldn't try to do the surgery that first time, just because of what *might* happen? Their world would probably be paralyzed if everyone thought like she did.

Zeke might die any number of ways. So might she. But did that mean they shouldn't try to grasp at happiness when it was within reach?

God. No. It didn't.

Why hadn't she seen that a week ago, when she'd freaked out over that plaque? Maybe because she'd never really dealt with the grief of her father's death. But what her mom had said really had helped her see it from a different perspective.

If she knew her father was going to die, would she have rather never known him at all? Or did those memories of all of those happy Halloweens supersede what had happened when she was ten?

Of course it did. She'd loved her dad with a fierce love that survived even his death.

"One more question, Mom. Do you mind if I head home? I need to find a way to get in contact with someone."

"Zeke?"

She nodded.

"Do you want his address? I have it on his mortgage paperwork."

"I don't think he's there."

Her mom frowned. "Where is he, then?"

"That's just the problem. I don't know. But I need to find him before it's too late."

"It's never too late."

"It might be this time, Mom, but I need to try." Shanna hesitated before adding, "I want to be more fearless, like you."

"Honey, I am not fearless. I just don't know where or when my road is going to end. So I want to do all the living I can right now. You daddy taught me that."

"See? That's exactly what I mean. I think maybe today is the day I need to take that leap."

"All I'm going to say is maybe try to call his cell phone."

His cell phone. Why hadn't she thought of that? "Mom, you are a genius. Thank you!"

She went over and gave her mom a big hug. "I love you."

"I love you, too."

As she headed to the door, her mom said, "Where are you going?"

She turned back and smiled. "I'm going home. To make a very important phone call."

Her mom held up crossed fingers. "Good luck. Just tell him how you feel, honey. Because if things are as bad as you say they are, that might be the only way to make things right."

"I will. And thank you."

She got to her house and leaped out of her car, making her way to the door. What if he was overseas already? Would his cell phone even work? Surely Everly Memorial would know if he was going to be gone for months on end, wouldn't they? Unless he'd quit. Unless he couldn't stand the sight of her.

She swallowed. Could she bear to hear the truth if it were that devastating?

Spending a minute trying to do some of the breathing exercises she gave her patients, she finally screwed up the courage to dial that number rather than just shoot off a text message. Like she'd told her mom, now was the time to be fearless. No matter what the cost.

The phone rang once, twice, three times. Just when she thought it might roll over to voice mail, he answered. "Give me a sec to get out of this."

Get out of what? Was he in danger?

"Wh-where are you, Zeke?"

There was no answer. In the background, she thought she could hear the sound of engines rumbling. Tanks? Military equipment?

"Zeke?"

The sounds faded to nothing. And still his voice hadn't come back on.

Her heart pounded in her chest as myriad thoughts careened across her brain, none of them making any sense.

"Okay, now I can talk. Unless you're going to tell me to go away."

"Go away?" She shook her head. Hadn't he already done that? "Zeke, I'm so sorry—"

Her doorbell rang.

God, not now!

She was just going to let it ring. This was way more important. "I'm so sorry for what I said in your office. You haven't been at work... Did you ask them to deploy you?"

"Deploy me? Why would you think that?"

"Maybe because if I were you I wouldn't be able to stand the sight of me."

Her doorbell rang again. Still she didn't move.

"Someone's at your door, Shanna."

"I don't care."

There was a pause. "I hope that's not true. Come see who it is."

Why did that sentence sound wonky? Shouldn't he have said, "*Go* see who it is"?

Come see.

Her hand went to her mouth as she stood with shaking legs and somehow made it over to the door. Opened it.

There stood Zeke. *Her* Zeke.

"But how...? Where were you?"

"I decided to take my own advice," he said. "Can I come in?"

"Of course." She stood aside and waited

for him to get inside before closing the door behind him.

"What advice is that?"

"I went home to talk to Mom. About whether she would marry Dad all over again, even if she knew what was coming."

Shanna nodded. "And she said she would."

"How did you know that?"

She wrapped her arms around his neck and held him closer than she'd ever held anyone in her life. And then she stood on tiptoe to whisper in his ear, "Because my mom said the very same thing. And I realized she was right. And I was wrong."

His fingers tangled in her hair and held her there for several minutes. "Not wrong, Shanna. Just scared. As scared as I was of losing you, just as I'd realized I love you."

"Y-you love me?"

"Isn't it obvious?"

She leaned back and looked at him. "No. Is it obvious that I love you?"

This time he laughed. "No. But you do?"

She nodded. "I do."

"I should have done a better job of listening when you came to my office. But I'd had a relationship end over my refusal to leave the military, and it seemed like history might be repeating itself. I just couldn't see past that. Couldn't think of the right words to say."

"I get it. And I'm sorry I made you feel that way. I did think about resigning my position here at the hospital, though. I wasn't sure I'd be able to see you day in and day out without telling you how I felt."

Her eyes widened. "Wow. I talked to Dan about working out in the community for the same reason. He wouldn't give me the green light until he'd studied it more. So... Here I am, making a phone call to you instead and praying I'd get to tell you how I feel before it's too late."

He cupped her cheeks and kissed her. "Obviously, it's not too late. For either of us. Oh, wait, I almost forgot. I have something for you."

"What is it?"

"Stay here. I have to get it out of my car."

Puzzled, she let go of him and watched as he walked back through her door, closing it behind him. It sent a chill through her before she forced her heart to calm its pace. He'd be back. This was hello, not goodbye.

Her bell rang again, and she laughed. "Zeke, what in the world…?"

When she opened it, he stood on her step again, this time holding a pumpkin that was flickering with light. And on its surface he'd carved a heart. Only this time, it wasn't the complex heart of his medical profession. It was a simple cartoon-style heart that sat in the middle of two words.

She read it out loud. "'*I heart you.*' Oh, Zeke…"

"I really do."

"I love you, too." To keep from weeping, she wrinkled her nose and tried to show him how happy she was instead. "But… You have to promise me you'll keep dressing up for Halloween. Because that pirate costume…" She kissed her fingertips and blew it away. "It was very, very sexy."

He went over and set the pumpkin on her coffee table and then swept her into his arms, settled them down onto the couch and kissed her shoulder. "I'm pretty sure your *Wizard of Oz* costume blew mine out of the water. But for now, how about we settle for you and me and a reality I never thought could happen."

"You and me. That is better than any costume I could imagine."

With that, he pulled her in for a long, sexy kiss whose magic promised to take them into the future. And beyond.

EPILOGUE

SHE HELD HIS hands to her lips and kissed his knuckles. "I'm so very proud of you, Zeke. Proud of your work at the hospital. Proud of the work you've done for the military."

Their relationship had survived his time in the reserves and had even survived a deployment. It hadn't been easy, and there had been bumps along the way, but she wouldn't change a thing. Not one single thing.

Zeke's dad had been able to come to their wedding three years ago, and watching her husband as he'd kissed his father's brow during the reception had been her undoing. She'd had to bury her face into his tux for several minutes as he'd stroked her hair and held her tight.

It was worth it. Every painful, wonderful minute of this thing called life.

As Zeke stood in his military uniform on his last day of service, holding their three-year-old little boy, while she cradled their infant daughter, she realized she could never imagine her life any other way.

It was true. She was proud of him. Proud of the life they'd carved out for themselves. And most of all, she was proud that they'd both been fearless enough to risk everything. For each other.

For love.

* * * * *

If you enjoyed this story, check out these other great reads from Tina Beckett

The Surgeon She Could Never Forget
The Nurse's One-Night Baby
The Vet, the Pup and the Paramedic
A Family Made in Paradise

All available now!